Hamlet's Planets

A Sandstone Book

Hamlet's Planets

PARABLES

STORIES BY
Lynda Sexson

WOODCUTS BY
Gennie DeWeese

*to Jacklyn,
between us,
a Dreaming
Pomegranate.*

Very Best Wishes,

Lynda Sexson

2000

Ohio State University Press
COLUMBUS

Library of Congress Cataloging-in-Publication Data

Sexson, Lynda.
    Hamlet's planets : parables / stories by Lynda Sexson ; woodcuts
by Gennie DeWeese.
        p.   cm.
    "A Sandstone book"—Half t.p.
    ISBN 0-8142-0718-9 (alk. paper).   —ISBN 0-8142-0719-7 (pbk.   :
alk. paper)
    I. DeWeese, Gennie.   II. Title.
PS3569.E8857H3   1996
813'.54—dc20   96-21115
                                                                    CIP

Text and jacket design by James F. Brisson.
Type set in Centaur.
Printed by Thomson-Shore, Inc., Ann Arbor, Michigan.

9 8 7 6 5 4 3 2 1

———◇———

to Devin

and

to Vanessa

———◇———

CONTENTS

ACKNOWLEDGMENTS

Acknowledgment is made to the publications in which the following stories first appeared, some in slightly altered form. "Turning" is collected in *Sudden Fiction: American Short-Short Stories*, ed. Robert Shapard and James Thomas (Layton, Utah: Peregrine Smith, 1986), and was originally published in the *Kenyon Review*; "Pigs with Wings: A Domestic Tale" appeared in *Montana Eagle*; "The Incarnation of God into the Body of Florence" in *Mid-American Review*; "Causality and the Clown," the *Greensboro Review*; "Causes and Indians," *Studia Mystica*; "Lunch," *Spectrum*; "Sunya," *SPSM&H*; "Forgery," *Black Warrior Review*; "To See a Mouse," *Manoa*; "Of All God's Creatures," *Mythosphere*; "Seven Deadly Skins," *Carolina Quarterly*; "Pupil," *Other Voices*; "Hamlet's Planets: Parable 2:B," originally published in the *Kenyon Review*, was reprinted in *Primavera* and *Montana Eagle*. My thanks to those editors and readers. My special gratitude is to Frederick Turner. I am also indebted to the Montana Arts Council Artists' Fellowship, to Gordon Brittan Jr., William Doty, Daniel Noel, and particularly to Michael Miles. My thanks to Ellen Satrom, to Mary, Sarah, Mother. And to those who are missed, Barbara, Shirley, and Bob. To my students, my dear colleagues, and to those who invite me and write me, whose deep encouragement helps make this work possible. The book's beauty belongs to Gennie DeWeese, exceptional artist and friend. Its existence belongs to my editor, Charlotte Dihoff. My reason to make things at all, to Devin, to Vanessa, and, every letter and space, to Michael.

Turning

THREE ELDERLY LADIES, elegantly turned with jewels on their elongated necks, helped one another to hobble from the taxi to the walk. They came toward the house, their white, curled heads nodding, anticipated by the little boy watching from behind the curtain. They looked like a motion picture of three swans gliding and bobbing on a pale lake, but caught in a faulty, halting projector chewing up the frames of their finale. It was as though these fine creatures could not be crippled; it was merely the illusion of a flawed presentation of them.

Inside the house they settled into Queen Anne chairs; prim but for their knees, which would no longer stick together, they looked like great water birds, forced not only onto dry land but into human forms which did not suit them. The little boy pushed his trucks on the carpet, making highway sound effects for their entertainment. He peeked into the darkness under their skirts, which was like looking into his View Master without the reels. They turned their heads from side to side examining the boy, like birds who have an eye to each hemisphere.

The boy's mother brought out a decorated cake with four candles, bone china cups for the tea, and a glass of milk with a strawberry in it.

"Why, this cake says 'Robert'; the cake has the same name as you," said the first old lady to the boy.

He giggled and fell back on the carpet. "No," he shrieked, "it's my birthday, Louise Dear." He followed religiously their pet names for one another, pronouncing them with formality and deference. They were Louise Dear, Olivia Sweet, and Ruth Love. Every time he said those names it gave them rare little reverberations of pleasure in their old flesh, like spreading circles on the surface of water.

"Why then," said Ruth, "this pretty box must be for you. It says, 'Happy Birthday.'" Robert shredded the wrapping paper and found a shirt bearing an appliquéd lion's face with a yarn mane on the front and a cloth tail attached to the back. Robert put it on over the shirt he was wearing. He got the buttons wrong; he watched Ruth's fingers work to correct his carelessness. Her knobby fingers looked like bleached, brittle twigs. Robert wondered if they could push the buttons through, not realizing that the lion had been crafted by those same fingers.

His mother lit the candles, and the ladies sang, "Happy Birthday, dear Robert," like the air rushing from leaky organs. Olivia gave him a package of crayons that willfully changed colors as they were used. Robert drew a picture of the ladies on the large drawing paper that accompanied the crayons. They smiled to see themselves emerge as armless, floating shapes, with stick fingers at the sides of ruffled heads, each finished with a distinct and careful navel. He gave the drawing to Olivia.

"We never expected to *receive* a beautiful present on *your* birthday," she thanked him. They passed the drawing around and cooed at it.

Louise gave him a package with so many bows it looked like a little animal. Robert chose to keep it as it was—not to look inside yet. The ladies laughed and winked.

He served them cake that they faced as birds would face seeds and crumbs smeared with sticky frosting. Robert waited until they politely abandoned the cake; he leaned into Olivia Sweet's lap, wadding her silky dress into his moist fists, "Let's have a story now." His mother gathered the dishes and left them to their ceremonies.

"This is the story," she said vaguely, "of 'The Emperor Who Had No Skin.'"

"No clothes," corrected Louise.

"No flesh," agreed Ruth.

Olivia's way with stories was to take a great solid wall of a story and knock a chink in it with one word, making it possible and necessary to peer through the chink to the other side. Her story, then, was already told; the chink in the old story was itself the new one. They had only now to find it out by playing it out.

"Once upon a time," she said, "there was an Emperor who had no skin. He looked like ivory carvings and cream-colored satin cushions all laced together with fine red and blue threads. The Emperor would have been happy but for two things: he wondered why he, alone, had no skin, and he longed for a wife. As he was very rich, very wise, and extremely handsome (the other ladies arched their eyebrows), he came to realize that he himself was a riddle. So he said that whatever princess should answer his riddle should become his wife. 'What do I want?' he asked. At last, a beautiful princess with golden hair and a blue bro-caded gown came to his palace . . ."

"And," Louise took up, "she said to the King, 'I have woven a skin for you from my own golden hair; just pull it tightly at the top, once you're in, by this green cord I plaited from the vines that cling to the church walls. For the riddle of your skin is that it must embrace you like a loving wife and find you like a vine finding its way round a tower—' "

Olivia, who knew that stories if not tended could trickle away, broke in harshly, "But the Emperor tried on the skin and knotted the cord and looked in the mirror. He said, 'I look like a mesh bag of nuts and oranges tied with a shoestring in this skin.' He tore it from himself and the princess left weeping."

Louise blinked several times in the silence until Ruth said excitedly, discreetly dabbing at the bit of saliva escaping the corner of her painted mouth, "But another beautiful princess came to the Emperor and told him that she understood his riddle. To be without his skin, she explained, was to be closer to the world, and yet without skin was never to feel its petty pricks and pains. And this princess," said Ruth triumphantly, "rolled off her skin like removing a silk stocking, so that she could be like the Emperor and become his bride—"

"Yes," Olivia intervened, "and spilled herself out onto the Emperor's royal carpet. It took twenty royal maidens twenty days, picking her up and removing her by the thimblesful."

Louise and Ruth looked at Olivia. Robert, hearing only the story told but not noticing the story between the tellers, said, "Another princess came."

Yes, Olivia said, "Tell us, Robert, about this princess."

"This princess," said Robert, "was red and blue and green and beautiful, and said to the King, 'I'm going to give you a good skin to wear.' And she took off the skin of her best and favorite and big dog and gave it to the King. The dog died but the King said, 'I like this skin because it is fluffy and because it gives me a tail to wag.' And he did."

"But Robert," said Louise, "that doesn't answer the riddle."

"Oh, but it does," said Olivia, to Robert's relief. They all waited for her to continue. At last she said, "You tell us, Robert." The other ladies knew then that the story had turned to one Olivia could not swim.

"Well," said Robert, "you know, Olivia Sweet, the riddle is that animals have good skins and people would like tails."

"There you have it," said Olivia.

"But," complained Ruth, "*why* was the Emperor without a skin in the first place? That's part of the riddle."

"So we could find him one," said Robert confidently.

"Insufficient, Robert," said Olivia. He sensed that she meant for him to say more.

"So he could look at the inside of himself before he got married to a princess?"

"Excellent!" exclaimed Olivia, and seemed about to soar into the air. "I didn't know the answer to that riddle myself," she confided, and the other two applauded the boy.

"Don't ever forget," said Louise, "to look at the inside of yourself before you marry a princess."

"And," said Robert, unable to stop the momentum of his success, "if you wait a long time for a skin, you get one with a tail." They laughed and petted him, but he perceived that his last answer was not as good as his former one. He wondered why, as he himself would trade off a dozen princesses for one tail.

The ladies rose to leave. He kissed them on their thin, powdered cheeks and felt how their skins didn't quite fit them and wondered. As Olivia kissed him she said, "Don't ever, Robert, look for morals after you find out riddles."

Squeezed into their taxi, they looked like large fowl stuffed into a crate for market. They waved their white gloves at the house toward the space pulled in the curtain.

Pigs with Wings
A Domestic Tale

A HARDROCK MAN came into this town of butter and cheese people. I didn't know where he'd been before. The snow melted and there he was. I heard his name was Cal. Must have been short for the mountains on the calendar picture. August. California.

===◇===

I walked into town and spent all my pennies on a different ribbon each day so I could let him look at me. I bought ribbons; I wanted to present a perfect picture, not be caught with something ugly in the shiny brown bags as big as mittens. When I had worked through the reds and blues and was picking out one the color of the agate on my dresser, he stopped me.

===◇===

At the drugstore someone said he was an escaped convict; at the post office they said he was with the FBI. It turned out that he'd been sent by the John Deere Company to fix the machinery they sold that was too much for our baling-wire mechanics. He smelled a little like blue-lustered oil; that suited me all right.

===◇===

He wore his clothes like rained-on paper stuck to stone. All my calm and knowledge gushed past. Cal touched my hair, put his tongue in my mouth, and everything familiar drained through me; he held me a stranger to myself. But it never felt quite like that again, but for once in the snow. It's like I was wakened from a fevered nap and made to stand up and hold still for a lot of pictures. First you're asleep, then you're made to hold still.

========⟡========

I went home to a foreign place and told them he would build me a house of my own. In a month I would be gone. Cal came to the house I had lived in all my life and sat on the edge of the rocker so it couldn't move. The chair was accustomed to having its own way with whoever sat in it; but this man pinned it to the floor with tense leg muscles. I almost laughed, as that chair had scooted me half across the room every time I got up into it.

========⟡========

My momma and dad squinted at him, then at each other; he squinted back. When he glanced at me there was a subdued ripple. It reminded me of a trained German shepherd dog I had seen once. The dog would lie still on a platform while an iridescent bird walked all over him and perched on his head, flipping its tail feathers. The dog tried not to twitch. I never thought before now, but that was a trained bird, too.

========⟡========

My momma set about to decorate the inevitable. That's what women were like then, or tried to be. My dad tried to talk. He sounded like the guy with the marbles in his mouth, practicing to make room for the round shapes of truth. I was always waiting for him to spit out the mumbles and get on with the truth.

========⟡========

But the words came out that time, too, like a mudslide. *This guy: his kind always leaves.* I didn't ever hear straight on what he said, not like when my momma talked, her tongue clapping against her teeth like a bell. With my dad, since I was a baby, I'd have to look around and guess at what he meant. I never got it wrong; we had gone smoothly through those early days. I looked up. He was right. Hadn't my dad said, *The sky has kind of wavy sleeves?*

———◇———

I had never known him before to talk about the world he saw on past the weather. And I wondered what the sky's costume was for; I couldn't tell if those sleeves were for my wedding or for somewhere dying. It was spring, I answered him; I said the lace comes out everywhere. Even in the clouds.

———◇———

Leaves a woman grieving, I heard him say. Lord, I thought, he must be getting sentimental; I had grown up and caught him by surprise. He wouldn't have expected it for another season or two. But I looked to the bursting and climbing of spring from the earth that we could suddenly smell and saw what he must have said, *Leaves are warm and greening.* What had been bare bones was thick and breathing.

———◇———

I whirled round and round in the yard for the last time, as I used to do when I was a child. I watched the green blur the blue. *All ways leaves,* I sang from a broken rhyme. My dad repeated the line as though it made him sad, *Always leaves,* probably thinking I'd never again whirl until I was dizzy, bringing the pieces of the world to one, but myself to fracture.

———◇———

When my stomach had settled back into that new person I'd become, I saw a crow come swooping in under the edge of its late afternoon curfew. My dad watched it flap. *Pick which fellers'll lie,* he said. I've

thought about that so many times since that first *Pigs with feathers'll fly.*
I never knew for sure whether he was blessing or cursing my life apart
from him. I don't know yet.

〓〓〓◇〓〓〓

But it had been so important to him; it was the last struggling thing he said to me at all, though he still lives down the road in the house that holds my childhood. I mark those words as his gift to me, I guess; and I'm still riddling them. I knew he was uneasy that evening. Way down deep, I think, he might have been uneasy about that granite man who had come to take me.

$$\Longrightarrow\!\Diamond\!\Longrightarrow$$

Cal did build me a house, and one to shame my dad's. Half done before my belly finished swelling the first time; all furnished from the catalogue by the third. Now I'm expected to sit in that house when I'm not rubbing it away with one or another of the liquids in the bottles under the sink.

$$\Longrightarrow\!\Diamond\!\Longrightarrow$$

Nothing has happened bad. Nothing has happened but the seasons and the children grown, and no one talks past them. But sometimes when I see the sky putting on its guise of lacy, flowing sleeves, as it is now, my mind clouds over, too. Somehow I think it was a curse. *Pigs with feathers'll fly.*

$$\Longrightarrow\!\Diamond\!\Longrightarrow$$

I was afraid of being like one of the fish decals in my momma's bathroom sending up cries in graduated bubbles. Blank eyes, angry mouth. Cal saw me once, looking like a decal of a flat fish pasted to the wall, dry and silent. He pulled me loose with one hard touch. Then I was cured of my fish stare.

$$\Longrightarrow\!\Diamond\!\Longrightarrow$$

I learned to breathe in this air; I grew legs enough to walk and wallow in this place 'til the spoons and photographs have stuck to me like dried slime. When I shudder they flicker, almost like unfit feathers. Or leaves.

$$\Longrightarrow\!\Diamond\!\Longrightarrow$$

Cal notices. But he's gone softer. He's been here too long. He's turning to cheese. I'm leaving. I'll write to him care of John Deere; I won't be able to recall the address of this place. It's spring. It's warm and greening.

=———◇———=

The Incarnation of God into the Body of Florence

"GOD, I REMEMBER when oranges came wrapped in purple tissue. Nowadays they're bound up in plastic. Isn't it just about time for me to die?" She heaved herself up from her daybed, "Don't you think so, Lord, Lord?" and the floral printed throw, faded by excessive time and thin sun, stuck to her moist legs until she unbent herself and it sagged to the floor.

To her surprise, God answered. He answered, however, with a question. "Florence, is that a moral judgment or an aesthetic one?" She was surprised that God spoke, but it didn't surprise her that he answered with another question. From all she knew about God, whenever he entered human history it was to throw in another question like a rotting fish.

"Lord, I'm tired," she said, aiming her voice toward the lace curtains billowing from the heat register. "You got nothing to do but roll around Heaven all day."

"You know better than that," said God, and the curtains stopped still.

Then the heat came on again and God continued, "Florence, how would you like to trade places for just one day? You think I should worry about you getting old and tired—well, just try to keep track of all that I have to do—and do I get to die? Never!"

"Yes, Lord, okay, I'll do it," said Florence, meekly acquiescing to the running of the universe on a temporary basis. She had been a Kelly Girl between husbands.

She went into the kitchen of her two-room apartment.

"What?" asked God. The voice seemed sharper, less like heated, fil-tered air and more like her slippers on the linoleum. "You'll do what?"

"God, I'll trade you for one day. You be me, I'll be you. But please, Lord, just for day—not night—I eat carrots but it does me no good. I can't see at night."

The hot water dripped in the sink, splashing onto the peeled skin of a brown onion. "How could you do my work if you think so an-thro-po-mor-phi-cal-ly?" God asked, pronouncing each syllable like a little spit of dropping water.

She patted her hair, looked in the refrigerator, said, "I hope you like cold chicken. Would you like me to make up a couple of sandwiches before I go?"

There was no answer.

Florence shut the refrigerator, noticed again that something was go-ing bad in there, went into the middle of the room, and removed her slippers. She spread her arms, closed her eyes, and swooned, "Ready, Lord God."

God, so repelled by the woman, thought about shutting down the Garden, flooding the earth, burning the cities, stopping the sun, send-ing his son, and embracing the leper so that the earth might be re-deemed, entered the body of Florence. And Florence flew off with the Keys to the Kingdom.

===◇===

God, incarnated in a flabby body wrapped in an old chenille robe, felt cold feet and put the slippers back on. Always the antiquarian, God chuckled at the chenille robe, took it off, and looked at the pea-cock on the back. As the woman's eye stared at the peacock, God imag-ined a celestial garment and the tufts of cotton became almost luminous and the design suddenly a marvel.

"Incarnation is such a problem. Where do I leave off and where does Florence begin? If I can fix up her robe, why am I suffering her indigestion? Why didn't I mend her body instead of her robe?" he

muttered through Florence's voice, and looking at Florence's naked-
ness put the robe back on. He wandered around the little apartment,
fiddled with her salt-and-pepper shaker collection, folded the underwear back from the laundromat, ate the cold chicken, looked for—
without finding—what was decaying in the refrigerator, counted the
money left until the next government check ($23.15), and opened the
closet to get dressed.

God felt depressed when he looked through Florence's clothes.

None of the dresses had been to the cleaners in quite a while, and the odor of Florence's armpits was an abomination unto the Lord. Finally, God decided on a green dress, grabbed Florence's purse, and left.

A few blocks away, God, walking as Florence never had, went through the revolving doors of a department store. With her charge card he bought a lot of peach-colored lingerie, a jungle-scented perfume, three dresses, and a ring with a secret compartment. God liked the silk scarves so much that he got nine of them. The clerks found the woman charming. Then God went to a restaurant, ordered and ate a meal that left only $2.15 for the tip, and walked home with Florence's new purchases.

The day was beginning to slip; God's own memory of himself was curled up in the body of Florence while he concentrated on the pain he caused in her legs. He took a bath, using dish detergent for bubbles, and changed back into the wonderful peacock robe.

Florence, as always, was very conscientious to detail in a new job; she ran the heavens and the earth with so few slips that the scrutinies of astronomers and theologians uncovered nothing. But even with so many of God's powers, that part of Florence that was present to the universe was weary and longed to die. However, the power of transference was left back with the memory of God in the body of Florence. And Florence, presiding as God, seemed unable to get his attention. The sun was an orange ball, descending dangerously close to the tops of the buildings and night. In an act of desperation, and of definitely human imagination, Florence with the powers of God wrapped the sun with a cloud that looked like purple tissue paper.

Neither the astronomers, the media, nor the theologians seemed to notice. Nothing special was recorded for that day; but an aging woman, glancing out a smeared window, saw the sun and remembered. And the translation was made.

===◇===

Florence wept. Back in her body, she wandered around until midnight, at last calling upon God. "Lord, have mercy," she whimpered, "why did you eat up all the money that I needed to last for seventeen more days until—Lord willing and the mail is not delayed—I get my next government check?"

"I wouldn't trade places with you," said God, with a voice that sounded like the traffic in the rain. "You just imagined it. I only wanted an answer to the question: Was your judgment on the oranges an aesthetic one or a moral one? Unfortunately, I think it was moral. I doubt that you'll be able to find eternal rest; I advise you not to wish for death."

"You should talk," she retorted as though she were reliving one of her long-dead arguments with one of her long-dead husbands, "spending all my money is one thing. But taste! All of the things you bought are garish or sleazy."

"What about the robe?"

"Never mind the robe. I've had that robe for nineteen years."

God, sounding like a siren going by, said, "Didn't you notice what I did to your robe?"

"I asked to die. You paint a picture on my robe and put me in debt. I handle the universe so well that no one notices. You! You can't even handle my life."

"Ha!" said God, speaking along the ceiling like the neighbor who walked with a cane overhead, "you should have seen the sign: the odor in the refrigerator. I sent you that as a sign and a reminder of your mortality and a reminder to begin to prepare yourself to die."

═══◇═══

So, Florence, contrite, lay down on the daybed and died. They found her three days later, beginning to smell worse than her refrigerator. Her niece, seeing all the new things still with the price tags, took them home and tried them on.

The niece's husband, a man who combed his hair over his bald spot, tried to make a condescending smile and a thoughtful frown with a single face as he advised, "I don't know. I think it's all right to wear things that belonged to a dead woman, seeing as how the price tags were still on them. But, I don't know, every time I see those scarves and dresses and underwear, they look like Florence picked them out."

The niece thought about it for a couple of days and then took them to the Salvation Army where she demanded a receipt claiming a tax-deductible donation.

=—◇—=

An old woman, wearing a plaid headscarf and jeweled bedroom slippers, grabbed the peach-colored lingerie and slid the ring with the secret compartment into her pocket. She was a familiar figure at the Salvation Army, usually buying dresser scarves and pocketing tea-spoons. The clerk watched the woman grope for her money in an old leather coin purse and noticed, for the first time, a curious, piercing look in the old woman's eye.

=—◇—=

Causality and the Clown

"She's fat as a cookie today," Jane says, looking out the window at the approaching grandmother.

"Jane," her mother chides.

"Well, sometimes she's flat as the wall." Jane pats the window frame.

"Be nice."

"I am nice." She kisses the window.

"Nice people don't brag on themselves."

"She doesn't see me yet." Jane watches the grandmother, with the smudged kiss evaporating between them.

On town days Jane, in her patent leather shoes, waits on the porch glider for her grandmother to fetch her and take her to town, one block long and two blocks away. Her grandmother always picks out a present for Jane for being a good girl, almost four years old and no trouble at all. Last time it was a toy compact and lipstick in a little purse; when they got home, her grandmother pretended to put the play lipstick over her already painted mouth and, admiring herself in the tiny mirror, asked Jane to look at her pretty teeth. "My teeth are so pretty 'cause when I used to walk three miles to school I always chewed a twig of dogwood. You do that you'll have a pretty smile, too." Jane looked at the big teeth and red mouth that revealed no wolf, but plenty of grandmother.

"Why didn't you wait on the porch? Your momma forget the time?" the grandmother asks when she comes in.

"I was watching you," says Jane.

"Was you glad to see me comin'? Did you get lonesome for me?"

"We cleaned my room," Jane tattles, "and we threw away the monkey."

"I do what little I can for that child," the grandmother says to Claire. "If it weren't for me, wouldn't be able to tell her from an orphan."

"What's an orphan?"

"Someone without no granma," says the grandmother piteously.

"Or a monkey," says Jane.

The grandmother brought her the mechanical monkey the day Claire said was too windy for Jane to go downtown. "She doesn't need something new every other day," Claire had asserted.

"Twice a week," the grandmother had corrected her.

The monkey had clattered on the linoleum printed like an oriental carpet. The grandmother got down on the floor with Jane and ruined a stocking. Jane watched her grandmother unhook the stocking from the metal and rubber catches and roll it down over her leg until it formed a doughnut around her ankle.

"Lookit there, I gotta run in my stocking. 'No need to run in those stockings, m'am,' said the fella. Do you think that's funny, Janey?"

"Yes," Jane had responded somberly. Dropping down to her stomach, getting eye level to the toy that was careening toward her, she asked, "Is the monkey funny?"

"Sure he's funny. 'Cause he looks just like some people I know," said the grandmother, and she wound the spring too tight. "Aw heck, Jane Marie, he's busted. Don't make things the way they used to, do they? Well, sugar, when you get to go to town with me, we'll buy somethin' that don't have to be wound up. Now, you won't fuss, will you? You sure are a good girl."

"Well, have a good time," Claire says. "Jane's ready."

"I'm ready, too," says the grandmother, modeling her coat with buttons big as silver dollars, her flowered hat pinned to her head with two hat pins, and her open-toed pumps with bows. "Come on, Janey Marie, let's us go to town." She holds out her square, red-tipped hand to Jane, raising an off-key octave, reminding the girl of the voices of the hens in the coop down the alley.

Harvey, the tugboat man, always lets Jane throw corn through the big holes in the chicken wire while the hens quarrel and make fools of themselves. That's what Harvey had told her. "Those chickens sure make fools of themselves, don't they?" Whenever he goes away on his boat he leaves his chickens and mail in the care of Jane's mother. Jane thinks about the chickens as they walk to town. Harvey had taken her into the henhouse adjoining the coop, holding her up so she could see in the nesting boxes until she found an egg. She feared the chickens would get her, but liking Harvey and Harvey liking his chickens, she tried not to let him know.

She remembered when he had whispered to her, sandpapering her cheek, "Looky, Jane, that old Henny Penny just laid you a big brown egg. Now just thank her and get it." The hen eyed them, switching the song of her accomplishment to a sermon on thievery, and edged nervously around the nesting box. Jane clung to Harvey and watched the chicken lift a foot, fold it like a fan, and then spread it out, long claws gripping the edge of the box. "She won't hurt you, Jane; just shoo her off."

"Her feet won't get off the box," Jane had explained.

Harvey stamped and the big Rhode Island Red flapped, raising acrid dust. Skittering through the little doorway to poise just outside on the ramp, peering into the darkness at them, she uttered long, throaty noises of complaint. Harvey dangled Jane above the nest and she picked up the brown egg just as the hen stepped back inside. "Let's go," Jane pleaded.

Harvey carried her into his house, where he washed the egg and dried it on a stained flour-sack. "Okay, honey, here's your egg. You take it home. Your mommy'll fry it up for your lunch."

"Are there any eggs that don't come out of chickens?"

Harvey crinkled his wind-water face, "You ask your mommy."

"Are there any eggs that have faces on them?"

"Ask her that, too. Bye-bye, now."

Jane realizes that she had forgotten to ask, as her mother had scolded her again, "Jane, you waste half the egg; you've got to eat the white with the yolk. You can't just eat the yellow."

Jane remembers indignantly that she'd almost gotten a swat for saying, "I don't eat the shell, either. I take that back to the chickens. They can have this white part, too."

Her grandmother speaks, "Honey pie, what're you dreamin' about? I swear, you're the oddest child. One day you talk a blue streak, the next not a peep. Well, what do you s'pose we'll get today? I bet we can find us somethin' good at the five-and-dime."

Jane's thoughts drift back to Harvey as she had seen him a few days ago, when her grandmother had dropped her home. Running into her mother's bedroom, she had found Harvey lying on the bed beside her mother. "Hi," they both said in cheerful, shy voices. "What'd you get in town?" her mother had asked. Jane showed them a matchbox containing black and white Scottie dogs.

"They kiss or fight," Jane explained.

"Would you like an olive?" asked Harvey.

"No," said Jane, "they like and don't like because of their magnets." Looking at the open can of olives on the bedstand, some of the juice, Jane saw, had dropped onto her mother's embroidered table scarf. "I don't like them."

"Go ahead," coaxed Harvey, "once you get used to them you always want them." Jane saw him slide his hand across her mother's cotton dress she had made on the Singer. Jane took a pitted olive and put it on her finger. Placing an olive on each of her fingers, she waved to them. And picking up a Scottie with each olive-tipped hand, Jane left the room. It was hard to carry the dogs by the olives; juice trickled down her fingers. She backed her way out the screen door and sat down on the step. Her olive fingers spread, and the Scotties fell to the porch clicking together. Jane dropped the olives, one by one, through the knothole in the second board, then peeked under the porch knowing she wouldn't be able to see them. She heard Harvey and her mother in the kitchen, left the magnetized dogs on the step, and went back into the house.

"Maybe we should take Momma with us," Jane suggests to her grandmother as they look both ways and cross the street.

"If she's a good girl, we might let her come now and then." Jane thinks of the monkey in the trash under the sink. "Well, if we ain't somewhere else, this must be the place," her grandmother says.

Her grandmother lifts her up to see erasers, pencils, combs, eyeglasses, fingernail polish, tubes of lipstick, embroidery thread, all partitioned by glass and wood. Her grandmother buys a hair net in a paper envelope, some henna rinse, and a window shade that Mrs. Wilson cuts to size for them. At the back of the store by the goldfish is a new shipment of turtles. A few are green, but most are brightly enameled with handpainted flowers.

"Oh, Janey, which color do you want?"

Jane looks at the turtles climbing over one another and chooses, "Yellow?"

"Let's get this pretty blue one with the red flowers," her grandmother says. Mrs. Wilson puts a blue-painted turtle in a goldfish carton and hands it to Jane. She carries the carton by the wire bail and feels the turtle clawing the cardboard walls to get out. When they get home her grandmother bangs around in the kitchen while Claire stands by the oilcloth-covered table, arms folded. Jane puts the turtle on the linoleum and waits for it to stretch itself beyond its shell and try to grip the waxed floor.

"Here," the grandmother announces her plan, "we'll put water and rocks in this cake pan and then set it in some sand in the lid to the roaster. Come on, Jane Marie, let's go outside and get sand and rocks."

Jane looks at her grandmother's high heels with the bows and picks the turtle off the floor, puts him back in his carton, and hands him to her mother.

"Turtles can't live," her mother says then, "if their shells are painted. We'll have to try to get it off."

"Now, Claire, don't you go makin' God's decisions for Him. We all live or die by the will of the Lord." She pulls Jane outside and bangs the screen door.

When the turtle is placed in his home, Jane pours her marbles from the little mesh bag into the water, tokens of a former day in town.

"What's his name?" asks her mother.

"Marble Cake," says Jane.

"I think," her grandmother quickly says, "Slow Poke would make him a better name, don't you? That makes sense."

"Slow Poke is his last name," says Jane. "People he likes call him Marble Cake." In the silence she turns her turtle upside down to study the spots and creases.

"The pretty side is on top. You like that ol' turtle I got for you, Janey?"
Jane tells her she does and receives a kiss. "Oopsy. I left my lips on
your cheek." The grandmother picks up her big pocketbook and goes
home. Jane runs to look in the mirror at her grandmother's lip print on
her cheek.

The next day Jane tries to persuade the turtle to extend himself, but
her mother tells her he is dead. The grandmother comes over and
scowls. "Claire, I've heard about people who wished someone dead
and get haunted for the rest of their lives." Claire turns her back and
wipes her smile into the palm of her hand. Jane sees the smile falling
out of her mother's hand onto the floor.

The grandmother takes a hanky with crocheted edges from her bag
and wraps up the stale turtle. "Get me a tablespoon, Jane. Let's go
bury it."

Jane hides her face in her mother's soft thigh.

"All right, Jane Marie, but when the Good Lord takes me Home, I
hope you'll care enough to come and say a prayer for my soul."

After her grandmother leaves, Jane searches the yard for evidence of
the grave. When she can't find where her grandmother had disturbed
the earth, Jane wonders if she had put it into her purse instead of bury-
ing it, for fear of bending, getting on her knees and popping runs into
her stockings.

When the grandmother appears the next day, Jane looks at her
purse. "You wanna go downtown today, Janey? I gotta get me some
unmentionables. Got my check. Let's go spend this chickenfeed." She
pats her purse.

"You got a hanky in there? I might sneeze," Jane speculates.

"I got just about ever'thing you could imagine in here."

Jane suspects she sees the hump of a small turtle distending the
leather bag. Moving stealthily toward naming the turtle, looking
around for inventory as they walk, Jane asks, "Do you have leaves in
there?"

"Don't *leave* nothin' out," snickers the grandmother.

"Do you have sticks in there?" asks Jane.

But the grandmother poses her own queries: "Your momma been havin' any company lately?"

"Are you company?"

"I'm Granma." And she pushes against the door to the store. A bell announces them and clears their memories for the labyrinth of sights and scents and purchases.

Jane wanders the aisles while her grandmother snorts and hisses in the fitting room.

Suddenly, her grandmother retrieves her, "Come see this," yanking Jane toward a very tall clown by the needles and threads. The grandmother thrusts her up too close to the clown and insists, "Isn't he funny?" Then her grandmother tightens her hold on her, saying, "Look," and points down at his shoes. The shoes are enormous, more than half the length of Jane; one of them is cut open to reveal the clown's toes—gigantic chicken claws.

"What do you think of a man like that, Jane Marie?" insists the grandmother. Her grandmother likes the clown; they talk as friends. Her big pocketbook moves gently against her, like a half-inflated ball. Jane thinks of the turtle inside, clawing to get away from the chicken man.

Suddenly, the clown apologizes, "Oh, excuse me." Jane assumes that he is sorry for having or showing his chicken foot. But the grandmother assures him that everything is all right, just fine. Jane looks closely for what had passed between them; she wonders what she had missed.

"Wouldn't you like to have a big clown like this?" The grandmother smiles up at him. "He can do magic. He's a magic clown." The giant, red-mouthed man leans down, drawing a nickel from behind Jane's ear, and putting it in her hand. "He wants you to laugh for him, Janey. He wants your laugh. He's gotta see your dimples." The clown's mouth droops. He leans toward Jane and peels something invisible from her face and jams it onto his own, making his mouth curve up

and show his teeth. "Lookit there, you wouldn't smile for him. Now he's took it for himself. That clown has got your smile." The grand-mother makes her shake hands with the clown, tries to make her say what she thinks of his feet, and takes her home.

It was clown magic, Jane concludes on the walk home, that her grandmother and the clown had used to steal her laugh. Jane's laugh is all gone and she can feel its empty space. Her grandmother has captured her laughter and will use it in secret with all number of clown men. If only she had recognized what had passed between them, the cause for the clown's apology, then, Jane thinks, it would not have been lost.

When they get back, the grandmother tells about her unmentionables, the clown, and the funnybook and Tootsie Roll she got for Jane before Claire can say, "The mayor gave Harvey free tickets to the circus. He's taking you and Granma and me tonight."

"Well, I hope he shaves. I don't care to be seen with a man who's not clean."

"It's awfully nice of Harvey to ask all of us," says Claire, looking down at the crack that was starting to cross the linoleum.

"Who knows what he's got up his sleeve? I'd keep my eyes wide open dealin' with that man," says the grandmother.

They go to the circus and the grandmother sits by Harvey, explaining that they were sharing one popcorn, Jane and Claire the other.

"What's wrong, Jane? Can't these clowns get a smile from you?"

Jane sees the faces in the crowd around her, laughing with their mouths open, full of popcorn and teeth. She gazes knowingly at the grotesque lengths to which the clowns go in order to possess the laughter of children. Between Jane and herself, the grandmother sets her purse, which seems to breathe and lean toward Jane. Jane jerks back and the bag falls through the bleachers and lands among popcorn and wrappers.

"Good Almighty Lord, someone's gonna grab my pocketbook." The boy in front of them turns and laughs, mistaking the grandmother for part of the circus.

Harvey chuckles, slides through the bleachers and swings down to the ground. Jane, Claire, and the grandmother peer through the slats. He retrieves the bag and swings himself back up, wriggling into his seat.

"What're you cryin' about, sugar? Granma's got her bag back, see?"

"The turtle will be broke." The boy in front turns and laughs again.

"Turtle?" the grandmother asks.

"The turtle's in there," Jane cries.

"Lord, Janey, the turtle's not in my bag. I tossed that old thing to the chickens."

The sirens and bleats of the clowns can be heard on the way home. Harvey picks her up and confides, "That turtle, don't worry. I planted him right by my back door. You watch and see if someday we don't get a red tulip or two right there. And we'll know he's down there holding up the tulips."

"I don't believe you," says Jane, rubbing Harvey's cheek. "I'm not crying anymore. But you can pack me home anyway because it's dark out."

=◇=

Causes and Indians

WALKING AFTER RAIN, looking in the sky for more, she circumvented puddles in the road and remembered her mother telling her that the Indians looked into mud puddles to divine their lives. She knew it wasn't true, but she didn't recall that it wasn't her mother who had told her. She stopped and looked into one of the puddles; she saw copperpenny Indians looking into mud-green mirrors of reflected firs. Nothing there.

At home her mother said No, Indians looked into bowls of blood. But disremembering is just as important as remembering, she added.

The rain came again, harder.

Later, she said to her mother, The rain trampled the pansies and tore their faces, making the ruined faces of the pansies into wet reflections of my own.

Her mother answered, Causality is a pretext. If you blame the rain you will never unveil the truth and the pansies will have drowned in vain.

Ha, said the daughter. If the pansies lived and drowned in order to tell me that causes are guises, that determinances are semblances, they have lived causally as surely as seeds, germination, sprouts, stems, buds, blossoms, and consequence.

The mother wished she could blame her daughter's father for her bad manners and faulty mind, but she said, You might as well know, you were born of a virgin.

Virgin births, said the daughter disdainfully, are glosses on history, etiologies that tell us how babies are not conceived; they are seminal

messages fathered on folk who need to know where they came from, where they're going, what causes them to be and causes them not to be.

Sequence is not consequence, answered her mother.

What is my origin? demanded the daughter.

Read it in the puddles, said her mother; learn to find the whys behind the becauses.

The road is flooded, said the daughter like a song. Because of the rain I'll have to wait until the sun dries the high spots. You see, every-thing is dependent, determined, derived . . .

You may as well know, cautioned her mother, that I am not your real mother.

You are lying, said the daughter, narrowing her eyes.

Yes. Lies are devices, strategies, metaphors, to turn you from the refuge of causality. They unhinge the claims of the causal.

Then, triumphed the daughter, they serve a purpose; they are hatched in order to have an effect—to bear fruit.

Fruits and eggs, mildly mixing metaphors is a minor lie form, said her mother, pleased that her daughter, in spite of herself, was coming around.

And as a gift, the mother took the basket of peaches and grapes, put them under her dress, and sat down on the carpet.

I will hatch these fruits for you, she said maternally, just so you will know.

You are only doing these things to cause a change, to have an effect on me, said the daughter.

You are looking at yourself, that's why you call me mother, said the woman, settling herself gently over the fruit. I am the bowl of your own blood.

=◇=

Lunch

"CHAMPAGNE. BUT I'M going to marry Jack, anyway."

"Does the lunch give me away? Tell you what I have the good manners not to say?"

"Yes."

"Well, then. Charlotte. You don't love him."

"You mean I should love you? I do love you, Samuel."

"Then marry me."

"I have to marry Jack. This has been worked out for me. A long time ago. This is what is meant for me."

"I'll take the offer in Vermont. We'll stay under down comforters all the long winters. My sister in Montana will give us one of her llamas for a wedding present. What more can I say?"

"You've never proposed before. You, me, and a llama swathed in clouds of goose down. Sounds like Heaven. Have you been reading those Arab mystics again?"

"Charlotte, I'm really proposing. Marry me. We'll be happy."

"We would be. And sad at the same time, like an Irish tune."

"You're upset. Don't rush this. Just give it some time."

"I'm prepared. I have been expecting Jack practically all my life."

"Charlotte. Let's get you in therapy. Not just anybody. Hillman's in New England somewhere."

"I'm going to marry Jack."

"He's. . . . He's a computer dealer."

"Yes, Sam, and he makes bunches of money. He has a master's degree in history of film, did you know that?"

"You're not interested in his money; you're more resourceful than that. Don't try to tell me he has a mind. I only hope he's a good lay. Sorry. I'm really sorry, Charlotte."

"Therapy. God, Sam. The times have changed. We've locked the door on the closet; psychology's the anachronism; everything's moved to the surface, we don't need the shrinks anymore or even our dreams or—"

"Charlotte, let's go to my place."

"No. Not unless you're going to make love to me. Not if you're going to talk to me about this."

"We are talking about it."

"Then we'll stay here. Have lunch. Lunch, you know is what it's really about. I see that now. I've never been to bed with Jack."

"I'm sorry I said that, Charlotte. I apologize. I don't want to hear anything about that."

"Don't be silly. What we say and the silences. I love you for the words, too. You want to hear about lunch? Why lunch is the reason I'm marrying Jack?"

"Sure."

"I'm not kidding. I'm going to tell you everything."

"Let's go home."

"Nope. Lunch. All day. All night maybe."

"I'm not asking you to tell me. I'm asking you to marry me."

"I can't marry you. Will you take me to lunch after I'm married to Jack?"

"You mean will we go to bed?"

"I don't use euphemisms."

"Yes, we'll have lunch. But you are not eating yours."

"These little bodies in a basket. Take them out."

"Let's go. You won't have to look at the shrimp."

"The waiter will take them. I want to tell you something about Jack."

"I've decided I want to talk about us."

"When I was little my father put on a uniform and went to the other side of the world. Mom watched the news and watched for his letters. And kept moving. I secretly read the letters he wrote her when she went downtown. Filled with mush and jokes about his buddies, those letters seemed proof to me that he was having lots more fun in the war than we were having at home. Especially since Mom was afflicted with the need to pack up and move every couple of months. Going from dingy house to dreary house, and I was always the New Girl. So I learned primary school subtleties of social exchange. Out of my sense of survival."

"More champagne?"

"More lunch. More telling."

"Shall we go now, Charlotte?"

"Wait. You have reminded me of how it began, why I'm to marry Jack. Suddenly, Sam, I see it clearly. Dammit, I'm not giving you an anecdote about childhood, I'm revealing the way we are wound in Indra's Net, connected."

"I'm glad psychology is passé."

"It's not psychological. It's cosmological."

"What does that mean?"

"The connections are subtler, more pervasive, more real than the old men with the cigars knew."

"They—not me, of course—might have trouble understanding you. Go ahead, Charlotte. I know if you talk long enough, you won't want to marry Jack. He's—"

"He's what?"

"I'm going to try to woo you, to reason with you, bully you, but I'm not going to stoop to making fun of Jack."

"He's really handsome, don't you think? Sam, do you remember school very well? Grade school? Third grade?"

"Yeah."

"Where did Jack sit in your classroom?"

"What?"

"You know. Who would Jack have been in your class?"

"You are trying to make me stoop. I'm not going to."

"You know, though, don't you? Now listen, Sam. That year we moved to a new school three times. Maybe Mom was trying to avoid the body bag that was going to come back to the States. And at this school I'm talking about there was no cafeteria. Each class ate in its own room, and for the celebration of lunch we were permitted to trade seats. The girls traded around, making maps of the daily social flux; the boys sat at their own desks, their knees knocking against the ornate iron, content to remain where they had done their carving and multiplication. The teacher sat at her desk, nibbling her carrot sticks and watching us."

"How much have you been thinking about this?"

"Not at all. But this is the point. It doesn't matter if I've thought about it. It's still acting through everything. Oh, Sam, please don't get cynical on me. Let's go to your place."

"Great."

"But first I want to finish this. The meaning and order of lunch. At George Washington Elementary it was not so much in the eating as in the trading. Each student would snap the lock, lift the hinged lid, and assess the value of the stock that day. Julie, who never ate, would go to the front of the room as if to recite, hold up her sandwich, and say, 'Does anybody want a baloney sanwish?' Since Julie was pretty and sweet, hands immediately went up. 'Sanwish, sanwish,' Roosevelt whispered, and could be heard all over the room. Social propriety called for Julie to choose a girl before any boy could be considered. If two or more girls had a desire to test their stature, Julie awarded the sandwich to the favored one, implicitly diagraming the social hierarchy. If no girl opted for bologna, she was free to display her favor toward one of the boys. Lunch was an elaborate exchange of tokens, cognition by cognation, the communication of social structure, and, more importantly, the communion of the universal order itself."

"It's a good thing you finished your thesis two years ago, Charlotte. Lunch would never be approved as a topic."

"Don't make fun. Every day at school this boy named George, from the back of the room, huge and fat, 'held back,' would shuffle to the front, blink from behind his smeary glasses, and ask, 'Would anybody like an egg salad sandwich?' No one ever took one."

"Never."

"Never. First, they belonged to George. He didn't know the answers. He was big and fat. He didn't make a quick gesture of it, fly to the front, make his offer if he must, and retreat. Instead, he stood there, egg salad sagging in the plastic bag, held as high as his Z-shaped arm permitted. And second, they were always egg salad. No one could eat egg salad; no one would take it from him."

"I doubt if even Julie would have pawned off an egg salad very easily."

"That's right. Don't laugh, Sam. She, after all, had been to Alaska and wore a real, white-fur parka to school, hooded, and banded with Eskimo design. Even that parka would have had insufficient elemental power to divest her of egg salad. So George stood there, elbow out and raised fist full of egg salad. Several people said 'Yuk!' 'Egg salad!' 'Ick!' David even said 'Puke!' one day, but Miss Coddington pointed her carrot stick at him and gave him ten minutes after school."

"I believe that's what you said about your shrimp."

"At first I thought Miss Coddington, because she was teacher, would offer to take it and eat that egg salad up in front of the room, just to show what was good for us and that she, for one, was not afraid of George's cooties, and she, like God, found us all precious in her sight."

"But Miss Coddington could not have risked egg salad about herself. Her hold on that room was too tenuous."

"How did you know? Well, of course you know. That's precisely my point."

"That Miss Coddington is universal?"

"No. But that, too."

"That egg salad was uncannily scatological?"

"No. But yes. But that everything is coded, linguistic. I remember one day Annette, brightly costumed from her mother's closet, was

performing before the class at Miss Coddington's insistence, so we all
might observe the benefits from Lessons on Saturdays. Annette leapt
and lost her slip. Her mother's slip."

"And I thought you were rejecting Freud. Charlotte, you protest
too much."

"It fell about her ankles, a heap of shameful nylon. But Annette sur-
vived the slip; when she offered her apple, one of the most common of
lunch tokens and most difficult to get rid of, she was able to get Tom
to take it."

"How do you remember their names if you moved so often?"

"If you want to talk about the nature of memory, promise me another lunch—after my wedding—and we'll discuss the mother of the
muses, whose name I can't say after this much champagne."

"She's not hard to say. I doubt you could spell her now, though. Go
ahead, Charlotte, tell me about school."

"Often enough, in the status games, someone would offer birthday
cake or fudge, to the enthusiastic display of friendship and loyalties.
I'd say, 'Who'd like the other half of my cheese sandwich?' nearly every
day, or, 'Who'd like this oatmeal cookie?' "

"There were always many takers."

"Yep. I manipulated the system and gloried in my power. I knew I
was somebody—or, I had to keep proving to my wretched self that I
was. When I held up an apple, it was a prize."

"Ah, yes, I know this story well, Charlotte. And, that's why we're
here, my sweet temptation."

"No. It's not simply universal typology. And though some of the
daddies were off at war, we made no connections with golden apples,
contests, favors, and battles. Certainly not with snakes and gardens."

"Miss Coddington did not tell you the old stories, Greek or
Hebrew; you had to make them up."

"Yes, but she watched, alert as a schoolteacher. Miss Coddington
caught Mattie spitting into her napkin. After school, Mattie had to
pound the erasers against the brick wall. Some things, though, she was
like those empty inkwells in our antique desks. Roosevelt had begged

Miss Coddington to call him Rose-avelt; it was his absent daddy's name, too. She told him, no, he simply didn't know the correct pronunciation, 'Rews-evelt.' One day I, prissy and self-assured, looked straight at her, sticking up for a momma's voice over a teacher's, and said, 'His name is Rose-avelt.' She looked at me, and although I wasn't from his neighborhood, she knew I was from his class."

"Charlotte, if you want to check my lineage, right behind those distinguished patriarchs are some buffoons. I didn't know those things troubled you."

"They don't, Sam. That's not why I'm not marrying you. I'm not intimidated by the odor of old Europe or old bucks. But back then, by correcting his name every time she spoke to him, Miss Coddington nearly disqualified him from the lunch ritual. But Roosevelt laid low, volunteering to take apples, a stale square of gingerbread. One day he was granted half of Shellie's ham sandwich, and was secure again."

"I see the game. Who took things from Rose-avelt Jr.?"

"He never offered anything from his lunch. He ate whatever he found in his lunch pail, so the test was never made. I never found out if an apple originating from his hand was translatable. I wish I knew now, but Roosevelt, living in a realm where his very name was disfigured, knew the rules better than I could have and didn't press his luck. He made himself valuable, though, finding his power by accident. Once, Timmy was trying to get rid of the third peanut-butter sandwich of the day, and Roosevelt said, 'What's that—an old *goober* sandwich? I'd take a goober sandwich.' It was a new word and one that Miss Coddington looked as though she'd like to throw down seven days of blackboards for saying, but she just twitched. Suddenly five boys in class wanted to eat something that sounded so revolting right there in the presence of the upper- and lowercase running over the top of the blackboard."

"Ah, yes, script, the reference for perfection, the model for society, the Heavenly Book. Is this what you mean, Charlotte?"

"Yeah, sort of. Then Roosevelt managed over the next several days to make other sandwiches suddenly funny and therefore edible. He'd

say, 'What! A *pig* sandwich!' and ham would be more desirable than
ever. 'What you got. You got a *hog* sandwich!' And bologna would
have to be divided between contenders. 'What's that, goober and
squish?'—he named peanut butter and jelly just to the verge of twenty
minutes after school, but though the tone was there, the vocabulary
was safe and Miss Coddington was thwarted. Girls would squeal in
mock disgust over the new names. Tuna fish was held up and
Roosevelt said, 'Whew! Who's gonna eat that old *gold* fish?' Tuna had
never been so popular."

"A toast to Roosevelt. And to you, Charlotte."

"Oh, Sam. You see. George, trundling toward the front, held up his
egg salad and Roosevelt sat, dumb as a post. Even cheese, inexplicably,
he had named snake."

"You told me there were no snakes in this story."

"Well, this isn't exactly a snake."

"According to your theory, I believe it is."

" 'That's just silly,' Miss Coddington had scorned. But snake sandwiches were far more pleasing than cheese. I could see Miss
Coddington was trying to figure out if calling cheese by the name of
snake could be grounds for punishment; if slipping into the absurd
was worth, at least, carrying her papers to her car for her after school;
maybe even sitting in the principal's office for recess. But Roosevelt
did not give a new name to egg salad."

"Was it the taboo, immutable substance in our midst, the thing that
even poetry could not touch?"

"What do you suppose happened to Roosevelt, Sam?"

"What happened to George?"

"George stood there. If neither teacher nor clown could touch
George's tragedy, I squirmed at my varnished desk and knew it was up
to me. All I needed to do was raise my hand, take that egg salad, and eat
it. Oh, if only one day George would bring tuna fish, even peanut butter and jelly, I'd do it. But what if I threw up?"

"What if he brought shrimp?"

"If you act like this, I won't go home with you."

"Shall we go?"

"Not yet."

"Okay. I think I see who George is. You're going to get me to feel sorry for him?"

"No, Sam. That's what I'm telling you. It was transformed into something quite different. From a false piety on my part to a kind of control on his."

"From the syrup of your piety you hardened to the brittle bride?"

"No, something changed in him as well. Not just me. Though I changed, too. I was disgusting; I Felt Sorry for him. I was the best reader, I got anonymous love notes in my desk, the boys stole my head scarf at recess, I had been to both Marcia's and Julie's birthday parties. When Miss Coddington made all of us draw bluebirds, mine, everyone had said, was best. I owned a pin that was a dog with green-diamond eyes."

"What a dowry. Will you marry me, Charlotte?"

"Hush. Don't. Could I have some tea, please?"

"Sobering up time? Coming to the conclusion of the story? I long to kiss a woman who has a dog with green-diamond eyes."

"No more. Gone."

"Aren't you telling me that time doesn't exist—or at least that it's more mysterious than mundane chronology suggests?"

"Mmm."

"Well, Charlotte, you assessed your power."

"I could choose George's egg salad and disrupt the game. That's what I thought. In the shake-up, he'd have to gain credibility, and there was cake often enough in our house I could recoup any temporary loss."

"You're a calculating woman."

"I was then. But it didn't last long. Every day I'd go home under my burden. If I could relieve George of a moment of that torture, his world, lunchtime, would all change. Why did I care about George? I thought I felt sorry for him. It was, I suspect, that a nice little girl like myself needed the world to be all nice."

"That George. What a man. He was an affront to bluebirds and dogs with green-diamond eyes."

"Then one day Miss Coddington spoke sharply to him, 'George, why don't you tell your mother you don't like egg salad?' Ah, I thought, I will be saved. The mother will change the lunch and the game will change. But the big boy said in a small voice, 'I do.' And the shame flowed over the classroom like a wave. All any mother would

have to do to shift the boundaries of hostility in the world of school would be to slip a turnip into the lunch."

"A melmac cup filled with macaroni."

"And really dreadful mothers would do that."

"One late morning, and a runny, not-quite-boiled egg snatched and dropped into the lunch bag as the boy is running for the bus. Fish sticks, leftover from a dinnertime power struggle the night before."

" 'What does your mother say?' persisted Miss Coddington."

"What did our hero say?"

"George said, 'She won't,' and sidled back to his seat. So then it was that Miss Coddington, as well as the cruel mother who sent those lunches with George, and all the kids who were picking on him, had to be shown. I would embrace the leper. Self-righteousness. My identity was at stake, too. I was a nice girl, Sam."

"A sweetie pie, a great kid, good as gold, smart as a whip. I bet lots of people said, 'I could just eat you up.' "

"Sure. It was, then, up to me to rise up to face this wickedness."

"Charlotte. You can embrace the leper, but you don't have to marry him."

"Wait. Jack is not a leper. For Christ's sake."

"Maybe plain yogurt laced with wheat germ, bone meal, and—"

"For Christ's sake!"

"—brewer's yeast!"

"God dammit. He's good looking, considerate, kind, intelligent—more than you think—very intelligent, funny, doing well, energetic. He has a great sense of color. He's tremendous on community projects; he really cares about people and people love to work with him."

"I wonder why I feel grateful it's not me you're talking about this way? May I hold the betrothed's hand in public? Tell me more about George. I think I like him better than Jack."

"I wonder now, if Roosevelt had said back then, 'turtle-egg salad' or slyly suggested 'bat salad' how the game might have changed?"

"You and I would be getting married. Charlotte, let's foil your occult history. Let's get married anyway. You can name one of the babies Bat Salad. Surely that will pacify your Gods of Desperate Connection."

"You don't understand. It would have been so easy for Roosevelt. What wall did he run up against? I remember I looked over at him; he slowly batted his eyelids and sat mute, half a peanut-butter in each hand."

"Roosevelt neither named nor ate egg salad. A man of principle."

"Everything remained static. William inevitably would say, 'Egg salad, ick!' Tina giggling derisively, every single time."

"Ah, yes. Simplistic opportunists, exploiting poor George just to put some steps into their own game."

"Yes, Sam. So, I tested my power again. I sacrificed my cupcake to the ritual."

"Who wants a cupcake?"

"Right. Although several hands were already up, Julie asked, 'What kind?' "

"White with chocolate frosting? Charlotte, I understand everything you're telling me. Ready to go home?"

"Wait. 'Let's see,' Annette said, prolonging the big exchange of the day. 'Sprinkles on top,' said Greg. 'Who wants it?' I asked rhetorically to all the waving hands. To the surprise of those who thought past chocolate, I bestowed the boon on William."

"No!"

"Don't ridicule me, Sam. At recess, just as I would have expected, William made a rush for my head scarf, even stood behind me at the drinking fountain and suggested entertaining things to do to Miss Coddington's desk, and finally asked me who I liked."

"I hope you said 'Sam.' Surely you didn't say 'Jack.' "

" 'I like my dog,' I said, and it passed for wit among the girls who remained loyal to me despite Tina's efforts to rally support."

"And poor George. He's still mired in egg salad while all this erotic sport goes on around him."

"What was it, Sam?"

"I don't know. Was George's flaw really a curse that caused the failure of imagination in others? Was that what made him anathema?"

"Even if your mother had stuck you with an old muffin, or you were unlucky enough to offer the fifth apple of the day, you were safe with George. He'd take it if no one else would. But that didn't secure him a trading position; instead it secured his station at the bottom. George volunteered for almost every food offered."

"But seldom was given anything unless no one else wanted it."

"Correct. Well, if Miss Coddington couldn't help George, surely Roosevelt could. But Sam, egg salad stumped our Adam; he didn't offer a name for it. He didn't transform it by language into desirability. And George stood there, steel-rimmed circles before his large, round face, with egg salad angled toward the American flag."

"No pig, no goldfish was ever in his lunchbox. I think I shall weep for him."

"But it's true, Sam. He never had anything but egg salad."

"But our Charlotte has tested her power, taken another woman's man, pinned on her dog with the green-diamond eyes—and goes forth to save the poor fat boy."

"Just listen. Greg even had the bad luck of meatloaf, and Roosevelt said, 'You don't say your Momma sent you with,' and he looked at Miss Coddington, then at the Palmer alphabet, with the look of testing the weather and changing his mind, 'sent you with *leetmoaf!*'"

"It was weak."

"But it worked. The girls giggled and Greg was able to give his meatloaf to Jason. George had raised his hand, too, like a big-tailed bird perched on his old-fashioned crew cut. So, I was resolved. The next day I was going to offer to take his egg salad."

"You're lying, Charlotte."

"Well, I thought I was. But, you're right, I didn't do it. Because that afternoon on the way home . . . George tagging along behind . . . right there on the street . . . I saw . . . I was mortified . . . a huge, chalked ithyphallic man . . . in profile and wearing only a broad-brimmed hat . . . beside a naked lady frontally sprawled on the pavement . . . with curls and dinnerplate breasts. Printed at the top it said, G O R G E DID THIS."

"Ah, the great sin of it."

"Sam, all this is coming back to me. George was confused. A little flicker across his face suggested that he would like to admire the dangerous, flamboyant drawing. But he realized that everyone going down the road would see it and he'd be blamed. I rushed in to stick up for him. 'You are dumb,' I said to Ricky and Greg. 'He couldn't have done it,' I said, 'because that's not how you spell his name. Everyone'll know you did it.' Ricky and Greg laughed. 'How do you spell his name?' Ricky asked. 'G E O R G E,' I recited, always quick with the correct answer."

"Charlotte, smart girls always set traps for themselves."

"That's what I'm trying to say."

"What did old George do?"

"Ricky just grinned and said, 'Hey, George, Charlotte knows how to spell your name.' "

"And George grinned, too?"

"Yes. Then with all the condescension one more school year and a whole year of living could give him, Ricky came close to me and said, 'Stupid. Charlotte, you are so stupid. It doesn't say George *drew* it, it says he *did* it.' Ricky and Greg screamed with laughter and ran across the road. I, with my wounded dignity and my Snoopy lunchbox, went home to my mother. Ricky had always been my favorite, and walking home with the attentions of Ricky and Greg had been the highlight of my day. Then Ricky yelled, 'Oh, George, Charlotte must be your girlfriend.' And George, waddling to catch up with me, said—"

"Yes. He said yes, you were his girlfriend. And you never forgave him."

"Yes. After this story, you'd never ask me to marry you."

"Probably. Good thing I already did. I can't take it back. Marry me, Charlotte."

"I'm marrying Jack."

"What about George?"

"I screamed at him. Right there in front of Greg and Ricky."

"And the chalked Priapus and his Consort."

"Yes. I screamed, 'I am not your girlfriend. I would never be your girlfriend. I hate you.'"

"And poor George probably grew up to be an ax murderer."

"I felt miserable. After my plan to bestow a little favor on him, he had ended up humiliating both of us. I really hated him."

"Me, too. I hate him, too. Let's go and forget him."

"I still had to do something about the egg salad. So the next morning I woke up inspired. I heard my mother and the clock radio come to life in the next room as I pinned my dog, glinting its green eyes, on my collar. 'You're dressed already,' Mom said softly. It seemed that anything could make her sad without warning. She pressed my lunchbox into my hand and my scheme suddenly made me feel afraid. I said, 'I'm sick.' Mom felt my forehead, but with her little maroon dress and high heels on, she was ready to take off. She said, 'No, you're just fine and tomorrow's Saturday. You go ahead now. You be good and I bet Miss Coddington will be real proud of you.' And she thrust me toward my fateful act."

"The eating of the forbidden egg salad?"

"No. I waited until recess, standing in the gathering mist like a wet chicken, with a round eye on Miss Coddington. When she finally noticed, I said, 'I think I'm sort of sick,' catapulting myself toward opportunity. She said, 'Well, you just go inside and you can write on the blackboard or read from the storybook on my desk.' The other girls looked envious as I went in."

"You ate his egg salad in secret."

"No. I put my cheese sandwich in his Superman lunchbox and was trying to figure out who I wanted to torture with George's egg salad, when I heard a noise. I ran to the front of the room and threw it into the back of one of Miss Coddington's drawers and then pretended I was reading her storybook."

"What happened at lunch? Let me guess. George ate the cheese without a word, without even a look of appreciation, or surprise."

"Sam, you are worldly wise."

"So what good did it do?"

"None. Worse. Then on Monday, whenever anyone went near Miss Coddington's desk, they wrinkled their noses and left. Miss Coddington, with a sense of smell as acute as her other wits, went until Tuesday before she even noticed and began to investigate, pulling things from the desk, piling them on top."

"Let me guess. She had: fingernail polish, postcards from Paris and Disneyland, a black, frayed bra, a paperback with a cover picture of the heroine fainting into the arms of a shadowy man, a box of Cheez-Its, all the pages of 'I will never again . . .' written one hundred times, little, grainy photographs of Miss Coddington posed beside old ladies and young men, a confiscated squirt gun, a toothbrush, used aluminum foil, stubs of chalk, lengths of string."

"Pretty good, Sam. Then, at last, as the children were compelled toward these revelations of the desk's secrets, she came up with the egg salad sandwich. 'Wow,' said Timmy. 'Look at that mold. The fourth grade has a microscope. Can we get it to look at this stuff?' Miss Coddington just sat down. Finally, she peeled her lip back from her teeth and growled, 'Who did this?' Then Timmy said it looked like it had been egg salad. 'Did you do this, George?' Miss Coddington asked. 'No,' he said, teetering in his certainty. 'I bet George did it,' someone said; but then I heard, 'Charlotte did it. I saw her.' My heart was beating so loudly in my ears, I wasn't sure I heard it."

"And Miss Coddington didn't even look at you."

"How did you know?"

"Schoolteachers."

"Then I heard someone say, 'I saw Charlotte when she was in at recess.' Did everyone know? There was so much noise inside me. But Miss Coddington was leaning over the putrid sandwich in the baggie, weaving her venomous attention around George. 'Did you do this, George?' she demanded again. 'Charlotte did it,' someone explained simply. 'George?' said the teacher, leaning closer over the sandwich. 'Yes,' mumbled George."

"Yes."

"'I thought so. And did you think you could get away with this?' old Miss Coddington asked."

"And George said no."

"And George said no, Sam. I looked at George, his eyes distorted to fish, trapped in the bowls of his lenses. He pushed at his nose, jamming the fish against his face. Then I whispered, 'I did it.' But Miss Coddington just kept on at George. 'And did you think this cruel prank would amuse the others?'"

"Yeah. Then she would have said, 'Look around you, George, no one thinks you're funny.'"

"'I did it,' I said louder. I really did, Sam. I think I did."

"I think you did, too. But I think you're guilty as hell. But I'll marry you, anyway. We'll watch what we eat. Did George ever know what you did?"

"Well, that day after school, Ricky said, 'Hey, George, the whole fourth grade heard what you did to Coddington.' George swam his fishy eyes toward Ricky. 'Yeah,' Greg said. 'You were great. You could be a spy and plant bombs.' Then they said, 'Hey, Charlotte, what're you starin' at?' And Ricky snickered, 'There's your old girlfriend again.'"

"And the joke was reversed."

"Yes."

"Male society, Charlotte."

"Indeed. George had so escalated in their estimation they suggested catching a snake. Ricky said, 'George could keep it in his lunchbox until recess, then slip it in the old bitch's desk.'"

"Not another snake in this story!"

"Then they looked at me."

"I would have, too."

"And Ricky said, 'Ah, don't worry about Charlotte. She'd never tell. Besides, she's your girlfriend.' And George looked at me and smiled, 'Okay, Charlotte, you can be my girlfriend since you want to so much.'"

"You committed the crime, George got the credit and the girl?"

"He didn't get the girl! He didn't even know he didn't. He just knew I'd put the sandwich in the desk. And he thought I did it for him."

"You did."

"I mean he thought I did it because I liked him."

"And you even went without lunch that day."

"Mm. Everything got linked, chained up, patterned. George got stronger, even though everything was based on misunderstandings, on error. And I became. . . . Chained."

"Charlotte, come home with me now. I'm going to tell you a story."

"What story?"

"I'll make it up. But, if you believe it more than the one you've just told me, you'll come to Vermont with me. Okay?"

"I'm marrying Jack. But I'll hear your story."

Sunya

A Woman Sings in the Hollow of a Story

Zen stories tell of a man who fell in love with an official's wife, was discovered, slew the official, and ran away with the wife. They lived as thieves, but the woman was so greedy that the man grew disgusted and left her.

He became a wandering mendicant. And, to atone for his past, he resolved to cut a tunnel through a mountain where there was a dangerous road over a cliff that had caused much death and injury. Before the work was completed, the son of the slain official sought to revenge his father. He found the man and was about to kill him.

"I will give you my life, only let me finish this work. On the day it is completed, then you may kill me," said the man.

As the son grew tired of waiting, he began to help with the digging. At last the tunnel was completed and the people could travel in safety.

"Now cut off my head," said the man. "My work is done."

"How could I cut off my own teacher's head?" asked the son.

M Y STRANGER MAKES a path around my house each day, his eyes brazening my window, my garden, my eyes. The wedding only three days away, I risk this one kiss he takes, he gives. Now I can go to the groom with a memory, like a book to read and read again in the vacant winters.

Since I have exchanged my mother's window for the husband's, I see my stranger as a small figure against my remote, gray sky. One day I discover in my tiny garden a stand of warrior irises, blooms all blood and gold and blue, where only yesterday there had been clean, combed earth. Their velvet reliefs, I see now, are a letter from my lover. He has come closer, come to work for the husband.

=◇=

My son is born with skin like a petal, bold eyes. The bearers of gifts exclaim the father has been fortunate. No one suspects irises are thieves, captors of my little garden space by the door.

=◇=

He breaks through the flimsy walls of my house, my mind, like a fire. My child, I cry, as he plucks him from me and says he will not steal a father's son, he must have only his own desire. He strikes at the husband, who falls against the candle flame, turning us all to ghostly theatre.

=◇=

He pulls me into the night and the rain erases our tracks. My milky breasts and our ravenous sex keep us wet and heavy enough for the flooding earth. Fire, then water, I say. Wood, metal, earth, he whispers, and my flesh rejoices in my stranger.

=◇=

Our tattering clothes gossip about us before we can think of new names for new villages. My lover, my stranger, closer than a dream, takes me under trees, holds me among cushions, finds me each time a warm, surprised amnesiac to that joy. Yet I do not forget my child, and my arms can feel how he must be longer, heavier. I listen in the night and I hear his voice forming words, making a language without my songs, my clucks, making a memory without me. The husband, I have heard, bears a smudge in the shape of a bird on his cheek, and his hand cannot close around knife or peach wood to hew a stake; but he lives. My child, I have heard, runs on little fat feet and wears a red cord tied in his hair.

=◇=

I have only taken a paper puppet but my lover accuses me with his black eyes. I begin to swell again, but my grief splits open and I bleed for weeks. I want a pear. My strangerlover steals money to bargain prayers for my health. He wraps me up and abandons me to go ring the bell, remove his shoes, slough off his sorrow. The monks treat him with resonance and rice. I am in the woods and I believe he comes to look for me once, once again.

=◇=

A rumor slips over the mountain of the husband's narrow bride who tends my son. I cannot abduct my own child: I must seize first a board to make a hut, then capture a needle, a bowl to make a home.

=◇=

I live at the base of this terrible mountain; I mend the victims of robbers, of stones, of storms. I bury the corpses unclaimed. I feed the robbers. The wanderers and mumblers in their robes come and sleep near my fire, sometimes grasping my bones as they dream.

=◇=

Though he says he has forgotten me, he still boasts he killed the husband; and the tales claim he will make a cave to atone. Yet, a cave will be a reminder of his misdeeds, a story in the stone for everyone who journeys near this mountain. I creep up the ridge at night to the hole after his first day of digging. The space he has carved in the mountain is the shape of me; he so faithfully carves his forgetting, I fit inside it, curves of my thigh, my breasts, my hair. I tuck myself into his space in the mountain and dream until nearly dawn. Now the

mountain, his forgetting, his atonement, and my flesh, my presence, my memory make up form and force equal to what yesterday was solely, merely, mountain.

=◇=

Just as his desire deluded him from its consequences, so too his atonement deludes him of its consequence—remainder or yield. He dumps buckets of dirt over the cliff onto my squash vines, weights the leaves of my plum, bends the stalks and shoots of my herbs. My work now is not only to garden, but to gather up, to remember our love by carrying away its debris, spooning and brushing the dirt from the green, banking it up and building an undeliberate, miniature mountain here at the base of the great one. How many years have we been at our work? Emptying, clearing away.

———◇———

I hear that my son has come, shouting revenge for the long-ago crime. He does not seek to kill his mother who abandoned him. Why break such a scrawny neck, scorched heart? My stranger's atonement is a lengthening, dark monument, an eye through the mountain, but what will he see through our brief love, our lingering grief? My spontaneous mountain is growing, made of the hole in the big one.

———◇———

They work together now, and my old stranger's load is lightened by that secret son. My work is doubled, as bucket after bucketful pour over the cliff onto my garden, hut, tombs. If they knew they were one flesh by means of mine, they would not laugh together in the twilight, bring tea to each other. At night I visit the long hollow, stroke the cool walls, and dance against the stone that my son and his teacher carve. It replicates the channel of my child's birth, my stranger's desire; they are cutting the mountain into a monstrous woman, though they have no mind of her. They hear me and fear they have exhumed a spiteful yin spirit, but they know they will break through the mountain soon. I leave them a basket of peaches at the mouth of their passion.

———◇———

The one-legged man, who moves so swiftly over the face of the mountain, ties strings across the entrance of the growing cave to keep the curious sun from rolling inside to test the void. My severe stranger and my questing son chase him away, failing to see they are kindred artists. They are good workers, my son and my stranger, never glancing at the topazes they scrape out of the mountain's belly and fling with the debris over the cliff, never glancing over the cliff to wonder at the destination of their rubble. I send the topazes to the bottom of the well of healing water.

━━◇━━

Finally, they have finished their work and have come down the mountain and stopped to rest here; they lay about among the travelers. They call me grandmother, and do not recognize who mends and feeds them. They cannot see inside me is a cavity, once a light, and once ardent enough to cut a window through stone. I tell them, if they continue to brag of their splendid cave taming the brutal mountain, I shall lop off the head of one or the other. They laugh at an old woman who cannot hold their story. My old stranger nods when I point at an iris, but his memory is empty; perhaps he is free. The robbers like the cave; it makes their work easier and keeps their wine cool.

━━◇━━

Son and his teacher, my bent stranger, watch pilgrims take the path by my house to look at the replica of the mountain. I climb the miniature, bind and trim the bonzais on its sharp cliffs. A mole forces its blind way through my small mountain, making a tunnel; my son traps him. And the big mountain continues to send me corpses and the injured with bleeding mouths and torn purses.

━━◇━━

Forgery

WHEN I WAS LITTLE, I inspected each dollar bill that passed through my hands. I examined my currency with exquisite care before I transformed it by the magic of commerce into erasers shaped like animals and pencils topped by wooden dolls—leaving enough change for a pack of play money that included its own change in aluminum coins. Or, I'd get ten comic books all at once—to read about Scrooge, who could hear the plink of a phony as he dove into seven feet of coins; the nephews who helped their rich uncle for the rewards of fantastic adventures; Pluto (I never knew what his name meant); Grandma, Wisdom in her electric car; and Gladstone, forever stubbing his webbed toe on diamonds. I was waiting to stumble upon that counterfeit bill that would someday wind an inevitable path toward my possession.

I longed for a dollar bill that was not a mere exchange token—one that masqueraded as legitimate government issue: a dollar that was not real, but was instead the work of a strange and clever artist somewhere in an obscure basement accessible only through secret passageways. His place would be filled with little bottles of fine inks, a bowl of silk fibers. My father said that counterfeiters could not master the inclusion of the silk threads into the paper. My counterfeiter, I was sure, could. His paper, at least as fine as Uncle Sam's, would have those threads, beautiful as broken blood vessels in an old parchment face, noble as the Father of Our Country solemnly hiding his fake teeth.

My father watched for silver certificates while I looked for sham Federal Reserve notes; the Federal Reserve issue, according to my father, was a government-made counterfeit. So, I came to understand how it was that my counterfeiter would rescue the Treasury from its own lie.

I knew, too, that when my counterfeiter's art came to me, by means of skillful study I would discover those hidden, infinitesimal differences between his personal art and that impersonal reproduction of the U.S. Mint.

My counterfeiter, my contrary artist, could not reconcile himself to the gathering of anonymous wealth, nor to public acclaim for his craft. He would wait for me to discover his genius.

Eventually, as I read the eccentricities of his note, I would have the map to his underworld of magnifying glasses and compasses, causing me to lose my way in circuits and optical illusions until he would apprehend me there like a wayward, telltale fingerprint. His genius for obscurity would meet up with my genius for discovery. I had been expecting him all of my life—but what if he had not been waiting for me?

I paid my toll into the city and noticed the sign on the booth that read, COUNTERFEIT MONEY WILL BE CONFISCATED. Was there a third I had not reckoned? Was this third someone else who was latent lover to the counterfeit man; or was it someone who admired me and hoped to thwart my attempt to reach my lover? Or, was it Uncle Sam wanting all the fake dough for his own collection? Perhaps it was the brother of the deceiver, in his secret service, standing between us to test the truth of our love.

"Hi," said the man in the tollbooth, making change for the ten I always offered. "Don't you recognize me, Ivy?"

Of course I didn't; of course he read my name from my open wallet. Great eyesight—he must, I thought, be the counterfeiter's brother. So, when he tried to make a date, I accepted. I knew he was forging our former acquaintance in order to manufacture our future one; but I saw the broken blood vessel on his cheek, in an otherwise outrageously handsome facade. I knew he was masquerading as a tollbooth attendant in order to snare me.

"Only," I said, "if you bring all the confiscated counterfeit money and give it to me."

He laughed, making a pretense of innocence and a date for seven at a restaurant just featured in the *Times*. That was to throw me off, to make me think he was an ordinary civil employee, taking his cues from the world that passed along his route. I was certain that he was, if not in collusion with my forger, a necessary test that I would endure in order to bring myself within the sphere of the dollarmaker.

He feigned to know me, but he would never have suspected my cargo of old, torn prints and chipped cloisonné that I would nurse back to semblances of perfection.

I wore green that night to remind him of our common bond. My only jewelry was a simple ring, my museum replica of an ancient coin.

He had a coppery mustache; I could envision him combing it with a little hand-carved wooden comb while he reread novels by Nabokov. What did we have to talk about other than the thing of which we could not speak?

He started by telling me I was beautiful, said with that peculiar grace of a man who is himself beautiful. He continued by telling me about trolls, which he had read up on because he was going to be in the booth for two weeks and wanted to be prepared for the jokes. "Trolls, do you know," he attacked the tiny, cheese-filled puff pastries, "have been reduced to bridge-minders. Actually, they are the guardians of all passageways. Psychic passages."

The salad was better than his folklore. Artichoke hearts, transparent slices of cucumber, a mysterious white root, a deep lettuce. The dressing had too much color, but was mindful of the wine. "What do you mean, 'two weeks'?" I inquired in a conversational tone so that he would not realize I was circling round to press him about the brother he had not mentioned.

"Well, I'm not really a tollbooth attendant," he said with ridiculous satisfaction.

"Of course, I know that," I answered defensively.

"You wonder how I happened to be there"—as though he hadn't heard what I'd said. It was no mystery to me. He had stationed himself in the tollbooth in order to bring us together at this point—in order to bring me ultimately to his brother. He continued, obviously enjoying matching the resonance of his voice to the expensive amber light of the restaurant. "I'm masquerading for my brother."

A spontaneous tear fell on my plate just as the waiter took it away. It was the first outward mention of my lover; it made him so suddenly real that I would have recognized his scent if I encountered him in an elevator. I composed myself and asked Buck, as Hamilton insisted I call him, to tell me about his brother.

He laughed. "Why? He's really a tollbooth operator. I'm interesting, because I'm not. We look alike if you don't know us, so I volunteered to stand in for him while he sends some good money after bad ."

"What?"

"Oh, he's just investing time in a bankrupt affair."

"How would I distinguish between you if I should see him?"

"I have a wry look. He's sort of shadowed. Very subtle—but I know you could tell us apart. We're not much alike underneath."

"Where did he go? Where does he live?"

"Never mind about him. We're not twins. The best thing about him is that I took his job long enough to meet you." He quizzed me about my work and pretended to be intrigued with the restoration of modest antiques. He talked about himself while I listened for a slip that would reveal his brother's name. But he spoke of his bookstore and I knew that he would soon confess to me that he was a novelist, boring me with the contents of books not yet committed to paper.

The waiter winked at me when he brought the perfectly cooked asparagus tips with a hollandaise that couldn't have been faked in a blender.

"Do you think," he touched my hand, "that restoring antiques might be a little fraudulent?"

"Yes. It's recalling an authenticity by means of duplicity.

Technique." He was pleased; and I suddenly realized how what I had said about my work applied to his brother's art. "Tell me about your childhood," I asked, hoping to hear of the other.

But the childhood he described was solitary; no one else populated his memory. I grew restless.

The waiter traded the wrecked asparagus for the fish. Setting my scallops before me, the waiter whispered condescendingly, "Ocean marshmallows." He was, no doubt, also a closet novelist; but I liked him. Serving Buck his sole amandine just as my dinner partner was repeating my name, the waiter smiled over Buck's shoulder as well as his own, and echoed, "Ivy."

"Did you bring the money?" I asked Buck. The waiter appeared surprised, and then appropriately and blandly retreated. His hair, thick and silky, was tied at his nape with a discreet black bow, ribbon and hair curved past his collar. The restaurant management let him get away with it, no doubt, because he did more for the decor than the potted gardens.

"Money?"

The scallops were good, not too buttery. "The counterfeit money confiscated at the tollgate," I reminded him.

"I left it at home, naturally. We'll go there after dinner." I felt a twinge of doubt; he wanted to show me etchings, and I was determined to meet the etcher.

"Pardon me, Ivy," the waiter intruded. "Telephone." He moved aside the gardenia, plugged a phone into the jack.

"There must be an error," protested Buck in response to my initial confusion.

"No error," grinned the waiter. "Intentional deviation," and disappeared.

How could it have been an error? Telephones appear like this only in black-and-white movies, signaling something significant. Perhaps, I hesitated, as the color drained from my face and the room, it would be Buck's brother.

"Hello," I said into the telephone.

"Hello. I've got the money."

Was it Buck's brother? "What is your name?"

"George." I looked at Buck, helplessly sitting before me, trying to look busy, spreading the stamped butter pats onto the wheat-berry bread.

"Hamilton is right here," I explained formally into the telephone, hoping he'd admit his kinship. Buck's hand jerked toward the telephone, assuming the caller was asking for him.

"Well, what're we waiting for?" challenged the telephone voice. The waiter's face appeared in my mind like the smile of the cat in the labyrinthine forest.

"What are you waiting for?" I asked.

"Oh, I just have this job until I get my advance."

I was right on both counts: it was the waiter on the telephone, and he was waiting to be a novelist. I was not interested in novelists. "Do you have a brother?" I asked.

"Yes, but he's a phony." We sent invisible smiles to meet in the wire connecting us.

"Have your brother phone me."

"Phony, I said."

"Phone me, I said."

"I did."

I hung up. The waiter reappeared, disconnected the telephone, replaced the plant, courteously asked if everything was satisfactory, kissed me on the forehead, and departed.

Hamilton was unhappy. He'd eaten all the bread, his fish, spinach noodles, broiled tomato, parsley, and he'd finished off the wine. To get more wine he'd have to contend with George the waiter.

But George returned just then, with a commanding-looking bottle of wine. "For you, sir, and your guest. Compliments of the gentleman over there."

We glanced first at our own reflections, then past the mirror, and Buck muttered, "Jesus." Surely that was not his brother's name, but it certainly was his brother.

My heart leaped. He was as beautiful as Buck, but, I thought, he was the real one, the forger. Buck had it backwards about the difference between them. It was his brother who wore a wry expression, whereas Buck's face was shadowed.

The waiter efficiently rearranged the table, setting two more places. I waited for the brother's companion to take the other chair; no one but the presumed forger came. "One . . . two . . . three . . ." I quoted, "but where, my dear, is the fourth?"

The brother openly ignored my remark and observed my person. No undone blood vessel graced his cheek. I realized he was not the one I sought. Neither he nor his brother Buck was my destined lover.

"My name's Alex," he introduced himself. Buck emerged from his silence, expending introductions and chatter.

The waiter came back, his costume changed to resemble the patrons rather than the staff. He took the fourth chair, pulling the little black ribbon from his hair, which he must have known caused his pale hair to gleam as it fell loose, and tied the band around my wrist.

Buck became sullen. Alex and George the former waiter took up an animated conversation like old friends. They took leather folders from their vest pockets. They spread notes on the linen cloth—twenties, a couple of hundreds, fifties, a few tens, and one that was a one-dollar denomination on one side and a fifty on the other. "Here's an old two, raised to a twenty," smiled the revised waiter. They released coins from little plastic envelopes and spoke in unfamiliar terms. Admiring the coins with magnifying glasses they pulled from pouches, they talked of trading.

George said, "Look. A Clark-Gruber ten-dollar gold piece." He obligingly explained, "Privately minted. The Goddess of Liberty's tiara doesn't say 'Liberty,' it says 'Pikes Peak.' And, as with many counterfeits, it gave more gold value than its official counterpart." Everyone toasted scrupulous counterfeiters.

Their illicit fascination didn't bother me; given my occupation, I am frequently in the circles of collectors, traders, connoisseurs, and bluffers. "This one," Alex confided, "is a Spanish glass; it rings like pure gold." A toast was raised to the art.

Hamilton, or Buck, the brother of Alex, picked up one of the magnifying glasses and peered at me. I tipped my goblet and looked through it, distorting my voyeur.

George and Alex paused to observe Buck the tollbooth pretender and me, looking at each other. A real waiter removed the plates of the glass-gazers and politely ignored the money fanned across the table. George the changed waiter requested of the genuine version, whom he called Grant, champagne and dessert.

I gave up my glass to the waiter named Grant and stacked the currency on the table like playing cards. They all frowned at me. I scooped up the coins—and tucked coins and paper into the front of my dress. The three of them turned their mouths up, thinking themselves close to the money. "These are mine," I said, and their mouths dropped again.

Grant brought the champagne. Another brought a dessert tray. George my false waiter refused both, pressing coiled bills into their indifferent palms, saying, "I know what's back there. Bring it out."

"Now, Ivy," asked Alex, "what do you plan to do?"

"Follow the maps," I said, placing my hand over my heart and the money.

"I'll help," offered George, "we'll pass notes all over the country."

The replacement champagne was admired and uncorked. Its label resembled the old bank notes. "Our purpose," objected Alex, "has been to collect them."

"Where is the one who makes them?" I demanded. They toasted the engravers. "Where is he?"

The dessert arrived. A Ranhofer-styled beehive, an absurd confection according to Alex, who pointed out the immorality of using false food refined away from nature to concoct mockeries of a romanticized nature. The other two plucked off little candy bees and pea blossoms, sucking on them as Alex droned on. One of them reached for my knee under the table.

I told myself it was simply sponge cake laced with honeyed liqueur under the confectioner's latticework. But when Buck toyed with the server, absently spying at me again through the pierced silver and tapping his cheek with the cool metal, I knew he'd soon plunge it into the beehive. I feared he'd reveal a dusty catacomb littered with dried bee corpses instead of cake. I went abruptly to the powder room.

A round, uniformed woman came in and gave me a note: *Yes, Ivy, but you have not met my brother yet. He's a much graver man than I. In loving devotion, George Scrivener. P.S. You see, we have passed our first note.* At the bottom, in a parody of ornate script, were the words, *You can be my Valentine, if I can be your Confidence Man.*

I slipped into my coat and out of the restaurant and into a taxi and out of reach. Searching in my bag for my wallet, I discovered it was missing. I studied the identifying credentials of my driver—severe photo, serial number, and a name his parents took from an alien tradition. But Benjamin, I was afraid, would never be sympathetic to any story that ended with "no money." There was nothing in my mad-money envelope, nothing stuffed in my coat pockets. I despaired to think of relinquishing one of the counterfeit items. The one I gave up might be the single authentic clue to my delicately gifted lover.

The coins, though, I knew were not my inscriber's line of work. Some of them were dull, weighted, crude pieces, designed to foil only witless machinery. Most of the others were forgeries of antiques. I removed them from my dress, the taxi driver's eyes seemed, in his rear-view mirror, to be floating in the night sky. His eyes and the sky were of a single dark ink, lit by shifting neon colors. When he stopped in front of my place, I spilled the coins, warm from my breasts, into his hands and raced for the door.

Finally recovering from the scrollwork of my delirium, I found myself home, alone, safe. I took off my dress and the greenbacks floated onto my bedspread. One seemed much older than the others, of inferior paper and eccentric shape, and claimed in eighteenth-century fashion, 𝕿𝖔 𝕮𝖔𝖚𝖓𝖙𝖊𝖗𝖋𝖊𝖎𝖙 𝕴𝖘 𝕯𝖊𝖆𝖙𝖍. That was not the one I was looking for. I set it aside.

Now the work, I felt, could begin. I easily discarded the bill made up from the front of a one glued to the back of a fifty. Here was an excruciating method for doubling one's money, especially considering the theatre necessary to pass them. It almost made me want to meet the artist; but I knew there never could be a profound relationship between us. Likely, it was two working in tandem, back to back. A man slitting bills with patient precision, the woman he lived with devising and enacting dramas that effected the exchange. Their incompatible arts made interdependent, a new Adam and a new Eve finding their way back toward harmony. I could not linger over that couple, I told myself. I had to inscribe the geometry necessary to square the circle on my own paradise, the place of my counterfeiter.

I examined the root of all evil strewn on my bed, these masked esoteric documents, keying my destiny. This alchemical gold had transformed mere arbiters of wealth into the radical touchstone for my own journey toward perfection. How necessary it was, I mused, to reverse the obvious in order to recover the hidden coin.

I suddenly perceived—Alexander Hamilton, Ulysses S. Grant, Thomas Jefferson, Benjamin Franklin, and Andrew Jackson all held their mint expressions in the face of my solution—the single one-dollar bill in the collection.

Certainly my lover made only one-dollar denominations. He did not seek wealth (make money to make money); he did it for the sake of his art and mine. It was only the one-dollar bill that passed through so many hands, the one he knew that thousands of hopeful children scanned; grown-ups, with wallets stuffed with twenties and fifties, seldom permitted themselves the indecorous luxury of staring at their own money. The brutal truth was that grown-ups simply no longer knew what money was, using the compounded abstraction of electronic notations. My artist had to commit himself to singles, the only bills that still beckoned the watchful.

I had the map at last; now I had simply to follow its convolutions until he should find me.

The telephone rang. George Scrivener said, "He has a dog. That's all I'll tell you. I'd tell you more, but I love you myself. I'd give you no hint at all, but I can't deny the woman I love."

"George," I said to the man who was still, apparently, waiting, "it's no use. I've seen his work. I'm on my way to him."

"I can offer you something just as illegal and tender as my brother can," he said, hurt.

I couldn't relate to George's silliness. I longed to reach his brother, whose refinement of tongue would be equal to his pen. I hung up and looked at my dollar.

What outrageous chances he had taken in order to send me his message! The changeling eagle grasped a branch with fourteen berries, and in his other claw only twelve arrows. One olive too many in his peace offering, one arrow too few in his war bundle. It was so simple; my lover must be going under the name of . . . Oliver . . . Oliver what? Arrowsmith? No. Less, fewer, twelve. No arrow. Narrows. That was it.

And there it was in the phone book. Oliver Narrows. It was too easy.

I went to the address listed in the directory. No such name was posted. I buzzed each household, calmly announcing I had an appointment with Oliver Narrows. "Not here." "Doesn't live here." Finally, one tenant said, "He moved, 'cause of the dog."

"Where?" I cried.

"Don' know."

I walked the streets, eyeing dogs. Would his dog look like the Great Seal? I went to the zoo. I turned from the seals when I heard a man call to a dog named Pluto.

Of course. My lover couldn't have named his dog Fido or Rex. By the time I realized I had found them, I almost lost them. They were far ahead of me and turning a corner. I followed, indirectly but intently.

I surreptitiously watched them descend into the basement of a building wanting paint. Pursuing them, I found myself in the furnace room with a polyarmed asbestos monster, then in the laundry, which smelled of mold and old rags, then closets—some empty, some bursting, then a storeroom packed with discarded objects that might someday find their way to me for my restorative attention.

At last I spied fingerprints on a wall—a removable panel. I moved it aside, replacing it before tiptoeing down a dim corridor. At the end was a door; a tiny, triangular window had been installed in the heavy wood. The pyramid shape was brightly illuminated; and I saw his eye watching me.

"Oliver," I whispered. "I'm here."

He opened the door. He held a nest of thin, silk threads. He caressed my cheek with them; my cheek warmed and he closed the door, heavy as a safe, behind us. Pluto kissed the back of my knee.

I saw his pens, fine points, his inks deeper than the Department of Treasury secret formulas; and I feared that he would desire to write inside me when we touched.

On Oliver's walls hung an uncompleted series of gorgeous engravings for a paper money that he testified would change the prevailing economy by elevating its aesthetic.

His style was intricate, tender, making love as well as money; but neither of us was content. Finding the secret, I could no longer trust the treasure. We both knew it was just a matter of time until he'd feel compelled to print up some of his fantasy notes and try to halt inflation by inserting into the world of trade the enduring value of the faces of his own money. On the reverse of my favorite engraving, in a depiction of the solar system oddly arranged, Pluto took his planetary form.

"You see," Oliver confided, while he traced my symmetries in the darkness with his stained fingertips, "this currency will not be bound by nation or the scarcities of metals or shells. I'll make enough for the cosmos, an intergalactic exchange system."

We forged our passion, but never faked it; we made love and spent ourselves, over and over. And waking each sun-gilded morning, he'd read the tiny creases pressed into my flesh by the rumpled quilts. "Before they smooth and disappear," he'd say, looking for inspiration for his more enduring engravings that would complete his great work, his universal money.

I feared that it had taken me so long to thread my way to Oliver that he had gone a little mad in the duration. Nevertheless, I stayed, spending his homemade dollars on gum arabic, storybooks, on fat little dolls for Pluto to chew; until, one day George Scrivener passed me another note, and I went out with some of the dollars and bought some thick, creamy stationery and indigo ink. I thought I would answer him.

=◇=

Pupil

"You're holding it upside down." Emily turned the book and smacked it back onto his knees.

"Can you read?" he asked, sitting in the dim light on the upended apple crate like a youthful shade come to mingle among beings of flesh.

"No, I just know which way it goes from the ABCs," said Emily. "Now hold it like this," she bossed the tall boy.

"Can I say something I'm learning in school, and you pretend I'm reading it to you?" Morgan asked.

"Is it what's in my book?"

"No, we'll just pretend it is."

"Okay," Emily said, settling into the wagon, whose red had gone to rust, pulling the hem of her dress over her shoes. "Ready."

And Morgan began to recite, one hand under the book, the other splayed on top, "*A man plunged into a stream to save a maiden drowning, her hair trembling in the current. No maiden, but a lost tree broken free and—*"

"My momma got me this book and she'll get me another one as soon as we move to Denver," interrupted the little girl.

"*—broken free and forced him under. A woman from the bank tossed him a cord, too thin for anything but hope. The false woman—the roots and branches—pressed his face to the rim of the water and held him fast until the brother of the woman on land came and carried him home.*"

"If my dad ever pays that child support we'll be out of here like a shot, Momma says."

"*Two bowls in the house. The woman shared her bowl with the man drawn from the abyss and fed him with her fingers. The neighbors looked in at the window and saw him wake and speak. 'I saved—'"*

"Wait. Hold it like this," she hopped out of the wagon and rearranged his large hands to fasten on the sides of the book like spiders. "So now you can see the words. Then it will look like reading."

Morgan pinched his face into concentration, "'*I saved your sash, too,' he said and pulled tangled grasses from under his shirt, repeating the danger—*"

"What's this story?"

"I don't know. Our teacher says them into a tape recorder from the books that get donated. We get points for memorizing and for vocabulary. I'm just doing memorizing. You want to learn it?"

"No."

"Let me see . . . '*pulled tangled grasses from under his shirt, repeating the danger, plunging again into spring flood.'*"

"Do you know any others?"

"Yeah. I can finish this one first."

"It's long."

"Yeah, it's real long. You get lots of points for learning it."

"Well, do you know 'Sleeping Beauty'?"

"I don't know. Let me finish so I don't get mixed up."

Emily sighed and said, "Can you pull me in the wagon, Morgan?"

"Wait."

"Wagonmorgan," she murmured.

The little row of tourist houses had decayed into dwellings for stranded transients, sheltering those who had misplaced their tickets to the horizons. With gingerbread peak and shutters peeling back to gray, each unit contained a single room notched with an alcove kitchen, backed to a bathroom with a tin shower. Little storage niches held the images of cleanliness and godliness—gray-maned, sour mops and cans of fruit cocktail—and doors that opened to the back field. Unattached steps that stood at each back door gave the sensation of stepping off a train. Everyone in the houses wanted to be off, but the slightest disturbance produced vertigo in those unable to go on or unable to die. Window boxes still clung to the house facades, and the houses clung to one another by back walls and sagging roofs, carports for the tourists; but the current, lingering tenants all stayed at home or used public transportation. The only wheels in these garages were on an old wagon and two shopping carts. The carports served as dank verandas, stained with old oil, furnished with wired kitchen chairs, and stacked with abandoned burdens.

"Pull me in the wagon now. Wagonmorgan. Morganwagon. I can say which way to go."

"Okay," he said, putting the book down on the dirt floor, and she guided him to the handle of the wagon.

"You were sitting on apples," she said, as his hand moved to the handle, swift as a shadow. "A picture of apples—you were sitting on a box with a picture of apples," Emily giggled. "I fooled you. Now go." And they bumped out of the shed into the cold, lemon light and onto the expanse of gravel. "Turn," Emily squealed, and Morgan stopped. "Turn," she commanded.

"Which way?"

"That way."

"Right or left?"

"That way." She finally stood up in the wagon and pulled on his shirt and elbow. He turned and she squatted back down in the wagon. "This is too bumpy. Go back the other way. I need a pillow."

He turned a wide circle in the gravel.

"No, no, you're going to the fat lady's house, you're not going to my house," she screamed. He aimed more toward the left. She looked at the back of him as he awkwardly pulled her, his blank hand stretched ahead into his spectrum, less varied than the gravel courtyard. "I remember when you came the first time. I saw you out the window. My momma said, 'Don't stare, Emily,' but I looked anyway. So did she."

"What did you think?" he stopped the wagon.

"I thought you were just playing or something, but Momma guessed and told me."

"What did you think?" Morgan asked again, trying to glimpse himself from that obscure mirror.

"I thought you were carrying a bush."

"You know I was."

"Yeah, when you all went out back, I got a chair and watched you at the back."

"What did you think?"

"I could hear everybody, too. Lester, Lester," she giggled.

"My dad."

"Your dad said, 'We stopped and got this rose at the A & P.' "

Then Morgan said, " 'Lookit, there, Opal, it's going to bloom pinky-yellow,' " startling Emily with his impersonation of his father.

"That's right!" she said, surprised that Morgan, the pale participant, had access to the drama she had observed through the back-door window. Watching was the daylight occupation for everyone lodged in the old tourist cottages; doing was work for their dreaming selves. Emily lived in the self-contained world of childhood, precursor to the self-centered time of youth. But her pupal self had entered into a rudimentary consciousness in which deeds or gestures, events or adventures, are but shadow-play for sake of the pupillary life.

Emily replayed the scene in her mind, while Morgan tried to construct, in his, the way she had seen it. Opal had lauded the rose and dug the hole herself. 'Lester can help with that,' said Pauline. 'No sense at all,' Auntie Opal had said. 'This ground has learned to give with me. I'm putting this beauty right smack in the middle of my patch.' And then breathlessly she had said, 'Now, Lester, let's have that hose over here.' 'Just watch this,' Lester had boasted. 'Morgan, you bring the hose over here and water this rosebush.' Morgan had found the hose, rolled up against the house like a complacent snake, unfurled it toward the sound of the voices, followed it back with the toe of his foot, and turned the water, gently, onto the plant. 'Now what do you think, Opal? Morgan's gonna knock that school on its socks. Not that he needs to go, to my mind. But we'll try it out. Try it out.' 'Watch out now,' Pauline had said, 'don't rub up against this rosebush.' 'I got five buds on this bush,' Auntie Opal had said, folding her hands over it. 'This is going to be a sight.'

"Want to go out back with me?" Morgan challenged, tired of pulling Emily in the stiff-jointed wagon. They made their way around the string of cabins, the wind sharp and moist. "I'm going all the way to the stream."

"Not supposed to."

"Want to come or not?"

She couldn't see over the weeds. "These weeds are too tall, Morgan. They're knocking me over. My mom said she saw a fox once," she confided.

"Auntie Opal says the foxes come in these fields to hunt. She says she sees their tails and the waves they make in the grass. And once in a while, she sees a whole fox."

"There are snakes out in the weeds."

"They won't do anything to you, come on." He made a gesture that snagged her hair with his finger.

"Watch out my hair."

"Auntie Opal says 'those curls of Emily's bob around as she talks—she's such a busy one,'" he mimicked the old woman. "She says, 'Emily puts me in mind of Shirley Temple.'"

"I don't care if she's mean about me. I don't know that Shirley. She doesn't live here anymore," Emily said. "You mean those snakes can't scare you. But they can scare me. It isn't fair."

"It's just that I'm brave. You have to be brave."

"No it isn't, Morgan," she explained. "It's that they don't get a chance to scare you 'cause—"

"You comin' or not?" he suddenly yelled. "I'm going. You can stay."

"I'm going," she said, and put her hand in his.

"Could you find the water all by yourself, Morgan?"

"Auntie Opal's never mean about you. She just likes to talk about you all the time since you moved in next to her. She says it wouldn't surprise her if you and I got married some day."

"Huh. You're too old. Besides, I'm going to marry this guy named Paul. I saw him once. In a movie my mom took me to. She wishes she'd married him. She even has a picture of him."

Morgan was silent.

"His eyes are funny blue, you know that, Morgan?" she twisted to look into his face. "You got funny blue eyes, too. Maybe if you got in a movie, then you could look out at all the people watching you and see them. That's what my Paul does."

"At school there are plaster busts of Homer and Milton. Do you know why?" he asked.

"It's too cold today. I want to go back, Morgan. The water's all bubbly."

"I hear it."

"It's in a hurry. You could drown back here my mom says."

"If you've a mind to drown, you could drown yourself in a teacup, my dad said once."

"Lester?"

"Yes."

"You ever see him?"

"Yes."

"I mean, did you really see him?"

"Yes."

"Then how come—"

"I'm leaving. You want to stay down here all day?"

Seeded weeds covertly attached themselves to children, sending the children on the errand of sowing the future.

"What do you do in your school, Morgan?"

"Schoolwork."

"Like what? Could I do it?"

He laughed, his hand brushing the weeds at his elbow. He yanked at a strand of oat grass. "Here," he said, pulling the grains through her hand, "describe this grass. Tell what it's like."

"That's what you do in your school?"

"Well, something like it."

"Okay. It's green and skinny." She waited.

"No, that's not it. You got to tell what it's really like."

"It *is* green and skinny. Skinnier'n you. It looks like you," she laughed and snapped the grass filaments up at his face.

He caught her in his arms; she wriggled free. "I'm the teacher," he said. "Describe the grass."

"Okay." She held it sideways against the sky.

"Finish your work promptly," he said, pleased with his imitation.

"Okay. It looks like little green birds with long feather tails, that someone killed and hung up on the line."

He felt for the grass and she handed it to him. "No, it goes like this: a hollow stalk," his fingers working quick as a knitter's, "spaced seedpods, oh, what's that word? Something like pale—"

Emily ran through the weeds. "You'll never find me," she teased.

He turned in another direction.

"Ow! ow! ow!" she screamed. "Morgan, a snake got me, it tripped me. Get me. Get me."

"Keep talking," he said, flailing and stumbling through the grass toward her, "though you're not likely to stop."

"Get me up."

He knelt to her, patting her face, her legs, "Where'd you get bit?"

"He didn't bite. He tripped me," she bleated.

"No, look, it was this vine," he said, yanking it from her shoe buckle and pulling it from beneath the grass. "This here," he said, threading the creepers and finding the blossom, "is a morning glory. No snake. There's no snake."

"Well, there was one. You couldn't see it."

"You didn't see the morning glory, did you?"

"I might be bleeding."

"Prove it."

"You can't see it," she pouted.

"I'll tell you what I'm studying in school now. We're studying things so small you can't see them."

"I can see everything," she said bitterly.

"They're called atoms and nobody sees them."

Emily pulled Morgan to the pathway, leaving the grass, *grass tasseled taller than the leap of foxes more supple than children.*

And the morning glories struggled toward the light, their tendrils binding the grass into bundles; and as the season heated, the grass would dry and the morning glories would set sheaves to lean and then lay, as scorched straw, back to earth. And the tails of the foxes would tassel in the light, and the morning glories, all green vines, would be silent pale trumpetings of a harvest sent only to the rotting fertility of the next grass. The morning glory runners, like farming serpents, would keep to the earth.

"I am learning to read," announced Morgan.

"Really?"

"Yes, it's little bumps—you feel them with your fingers."

"I don't believe you."

"Yes. It's true."

"Like goose bumps?"

"Yes. Like that."

"Can you read my arm? I'm cold." She slid her arm into the funnel of his hand. He carefully ran the tips of his fingers along her arm, over and over. "What does it say?"

"Shh. I'm reading."

"Are there pictures, too? What'd it say?" she asked when he quit.

"I don't know. It disappeared."

"I'll be cold again in a minute. Just tell me some of what it said."

"I read the letters M E."

"Emily!"

"No, it must have been *mermaid,* but it was disappearing."

"It says *mermaid?* Is that my arm's name?"

"No. It's something your arm has to say."

"I wish you could read better," Emily complained.

"I haven't been studying it very long and your bumps lay down practically as soon as I touch them," he defended himself.

"Why did you wait 'til you're so big?"

"My folks never heard of such a school. Then they thought Auntie Opal was just trying to take me away from them."

"Was she?"

"Maybe. Since I'm too far to go home, I have to come to her place on weekends."

"Hey, you darlings!" Opal called across to them. "Come back in the yard and have something to eat. I made you something good."

"Okay," Morgan hollered back. "Now watch where you step so you don't fall again," he said softly to Emily, spending the pennies of the language, smooth on his tongue, too.

Against the backs of the cottages were a tub, a rotting crate, rocks, bold clumps of dandelions, twisted metal, and shepherd's purse and chamomile holding off the enigmatic grasses and brambles hiding the stream, the snakes, and the foxes. But in front of one little door was a tiny plot of lawn, a delicate, shivering tree, and flower beds wide as graves: Opal's garden, incongruously set against the entropy of the other households, the harsh gravel on one boundary and the wild encroachment on the other.

"I made you a picnic even though it's cool. Emily, where's your sweater?"

"I never get cold," Emily answered.

"Lookit here, I want you to look at this," Opal said to them. "Remember when that awful frost came out of its season and crimped up my rose, made it all brown and dry, and I thought it was gonna die for sure. But I got out here, remember, Emily? I got out here and trimmed off all the frost-kill with my shears. Now lookit this, it's gone bushy as an old man's eyebrow and a young squirrel's tail."

Emily said to Morgan, "We got oatmeal cookies," looking at the picnic Opal had spread out on a cloth on her lawn.

"There's something crazy about my rosebush. I want you to lookit this." Morgan moved near Opal, listening. "It's come to blossom, and I haven't been really looking. What sort of devilish trick do you suppose has been pulled on me?" Morgan put his hand delicately toward the bush and she guided it into the clusters of white, small, five-petaled blossoms. "I was just separating the weeds from my intentions, but come smack up against, Lord, what is this?"

"What is this?" repeated Morgan.

"That's what you got, all right. All over it. Not enough for a pie, but there's going to be a good sized dishful."

"Berry," said Morgan.

"Blackberry," said Opal. "It really, I swear, was a rosebush, with most rare, pinky-yellow buds. Now what on God's green earth has passed through my yard in the night?"

"Snakes," said Emily, sitting crosslegged on the lunch cloth.

"What came with that frost?" Opal asked the borders of her garden.

"I bet the foxes came in here," said Emily.

"That's just like the tulips," Opal said in wonderment. "Some time back, I got tulip bulbs at Woolworth's. The pictures was blue and purple, like none I had seen. And that's just how they come up. Big cups that could hold the rain for half the afternoon. They was something. But you look at that tulip bed now. Do you ever see blue or purple springing up nowdays? No, sir, they just come up red, red, red, like tulips always did when I was a child."

"Grafting," said Morgan, finding Emily and folding himself up to sit by her on the lawn, "grafting." He said it again to his own immense pleasure, but noticed by neither Emily nor Opal.

"Everything shows you change," said Opal, talking to the invisible force that had confused her. "But the change is going backward to the way things were. People die and the plants go back to the weeds. You may as well just let them climb right back up to the back door, 'cause they're going to take over anyway. Someone, I tell you." She sat on a little wooden stool, "I'll just sit here while you children take your lunch. Someone, I tell you, has showed Mr. Darwin the door."

"The rose shoots were grafted onto a blackberry root and the graftings were lost in the freeze," said Morgan, and Emily put a cookie in the mouth of the unsung detective.

"Let's eat the cookies first," said Emily.

"Don't you eat those cookies first," Opal chuckled. "Well, I guess it'd be all right, long as you eat up the wings and coleslaw, too. I guess God give a goose which goes first."

They ate and Opal talked. "It's like I say, there's something peculiar round this yard, and maybe round this whole earth. With this cold spell. Things as they are. It should be hot enough for shirtsleeves by now. It's getting so you can't depend on nothing, not even. . . . You know, you shouldn't overspend your welcome on earth, and that's just what I've done. If you're past time, then the things themselves, all the whole place, begins to look like it's crazy."

Emily spilled her milk into the lawn and looked guiltily toward Opal.

"Never you mind. I think this whole place is coming to an end. But never mind those things, you two. Go play while you can. Emily, your momma'll be home from the café pretty soon."

"Can I give a cookie to the foxes?" asked Emily.

"Foxes may as well be eating cookies and drinking tea," said Opal.

Emily threw a cookie into the weeds. "You threw it, but it didn't go far, did it?" Morgan teased her.

They helped Opal carry the dishes back in the house and then wandered back to the dim shed joining the cottages. Morgan sought his wooden box against the wall.

"Hey, Morgan, let's look in this old stuff. Momma says not to get into it."

"Okay."

"Here. Put your hands up there, now lift that down."

He put the cardboard box between them. "It smells wet."

"It's not wet. You open it, I'm too scared."

"Why?"

" 'Cause there might be something scary in there."

"Doesn't scare me. But it's not like you think, Emily. It's not the same to me open as closed. That's not why it doesn't scare me. Closed is not the same as open to me."

"Open it. Hurry up, Morganwagon."

"Paper and clothing," he deciphered the contents.

"A shirt. And letters. This one's for me. It might have my name on it. No, it's in the other kind of writing," she dropped it on the ground and found one printed. "It is almost for me. E L M E R and some more. That's almost my name. Like on my arm. In the goosebump writing."

"No," he laughed. "This one, then, is to me." He pulled out a thick, rust-marked envelope.

"You got a birthday card," said Emily. "Is that really true, Morgan, that you can read bumps?"

"What's the picture on the card?" he asked, handing it to her.

"A little yard. What Auntie Opal's trying to make out back."

"Maybe it's the way Auntie Opal thinks her garden is; in her eyes it's like that," explained Morgan.

"No, she sees okay."

"Look, Emily, look what else I got in my envelope."

"Did you really? Are you going to keep it? What is it?"

"It's a silver dollar."

"How do you know?" she asked peevishly, pinching her letter and shaking it.

"Next year, I'll get to send letters myself, from school. I'll send you one."

"I'll be in Denver."

"I'll send it to Denver."

"Then, as soon as I learn to read, I'll read it and read it."

"I'll send you this dollar."

"And then I'll send it to you."

And out back, the morning glories, nearly as wise and pretending the part of serpents, worked at clearing the grasses from the wild vista where the foxes leapt, foxes who were wilder and wiser than the vines or the grasses.

══◇══

Irreconcilable Mutations

Y EARS AGO AND years from now, frogs take up the forest.

Where are they now, but kissed into slender and purpled forms of eager wishes? We want to know.

They pose on the dry, marble steps of the palaces. These princes are patient, waiting for the women to want to come happily ever after them. In the pleated webs of royalty, the princes have constricted their vaulting legs, their fly-swift tongues, bulging throats. Despite their moiré coats, fastened by knots of braided calligraphy, they sometimes feel all head and tail and water.

Where are the women? We want to know.

By the walls, the women lean close to one another, jeweled bosoms, blossoms in their hair, and whisper all their fear: if from frog to prince in a kiss, what will a kissed prince unveil?

They make vows of chastity, seals for their nuzzly lips. To keep their minds made up and their bodices buttoned, the daughters exchange an oath, with a kiss.

We want to know, can anyone kissed be absolved?

All kisses transmute.

The sisters kiss promises to one another, promises to yield to no more amphibiate favor.

But their fathers, from their high glazed and leaded views, they witness the oaths, the exchanges. And their fingers lock on the window ledges. From the easy and open pledges, the princesses at once spring up as graceful limbs and cinnamon fur. They abandon their gowns in heaps and bound over the walls as leaping, brown-eyed deer.

Can a frog, we want to know, whisper to a deer? Can a deer dream

of a frog? Is it to forget a kiss or a wish for a kiss that transforms the forest?

But, we want to know, do we desire prince, or frog, or kiss, or water?

Genteel conceit dissolves and the young men drown themselves back to tadpoles.

After many thin dreams, they remember legs, lungs, land. Frogs draw concentric circles on the pond again.

They sing in the night, on the logs, in the trees, by the water, recalling the desires of women who would open their mouths to kiss for the taste of the pond or for the sake of bitter fathers.

The deer flick their tongues in the water and bound back into shadow.

But what do the deer desire? We want to know. Deer, too, inhabit the forest.

=◇=

To See a Mouse

When Virgil sat down in the shade, leaning his back to the back of the house, an infant wind pressed an envelope against his sleeve. Yellowed and textured through a cycle of rain and sun, ink and stamp washed away, the envelope was a place to pass time on; so taking a pen from his pocket, Virgil made a V. On the point of that V he smudged a nose, then he spiraled ears, curved a back, meandered a tail, tipped little feet, and made two compact scribbles with lashes. He drew a mouse. He ornamented it with spots and tried to give the mouse a smile. The paper blew from his knee, and upon skimming the ground became a real mouse.

Virgil blinked and watched the mouse sniff about the withering nasturtiums and snapdragons, then scratch his way under the porch, trailing his extravagant tail.

"Might as well be reported by the tree that falls in the forest," said Virgil aloud. Just as no one was there to hear Virgil, no one else was there to behold the transformation of paper to mouse, nor to see his miraculous mouse go about. "A miracle without witnesses is lighting a match without a candle, a brief flame to nothing and still blind in the dark. Look at it this way," Virgil considered to himself, "there's nothing spectacular about gossip, but that's what makes a miracle go. It wasn't that the multitude got fed and full from a couple of loaves and a few fishes; the miracle was that those five thousand never got tired of telling it. Braggarts who were there and liars who wished they were, that was the miracle. Otherwise, with no witnesses, it's no more trouble than a dream. Hell, Mouse, I might as well have dreamed you,"

he called toward the foundation of the house and moved his hammer
and little cup of nails to a porch step, abandoning his efforts to block
the fitful gusts of wind.

"Maybe it's just as well Reba's not here. Her nor anyone else," he
said after a pause.

The spotted mouse came out, sat on its haunches, and sniffed.

"If I could see Reba now, that's what I'd tell her. I just don't like being crowded here with loneliness and misery. It's not Reba I miss, I just want her to come and clear out her sisters—old Misery, Miss Loneliness. And maybe she'd set a mousetrap," he said toward the porch again.

An old taxicab came down the road, raising dust, stopping at the end of Virgil's long driveway. Its dome-light glowed like a glob of amber with an ancient insect caught in it. The door opened and illuminated a woman on high heels sliding out of the car. Virgil remained in the shade, watching her lean into the wind that clung to the rutted path, watching her pick her way through mud puddles and jagged stones.

"Reba," Virgil said softly as she started to climb the porch.

She squinted down at him. "Didn't you know I was coming?"

"I saw that taxi hired out of Hell. Or else Heaven. One or the other."

"Why didn't you come to meet me at the station?"

"If I'd a known you were coming I'd a baked a cake."

"You didn't get my letter?" She kicked over the nails. "Oops. Are you going to kiss me? Looks like everything could use a nail or two. How can this place be so dusty and have mud puddles all over?"

"Those potholes hold the rain three or four days—everything else goes dry fast. Storm comes through and leaves these cool bowls of water for the creatures. Come down here and sit in the shade with me, Reba."

"I've about wrecked these shoes. Oh, Virgil. Here I am."

"Let's spoil that fine dress."

She came to sit beside him, desire traded on their memories, and they spoiled her dress.

Reba went into the house for a glass of water. Virgil felt in his pockets, and finding a sales receipt, he experimented. He made a V again. Then he drew a picture of himself: swimming fish for eyes, an unrolling scroll of a nose, loops of hair, a crescent-moon mouth. And to make sure, he printed VIRGIL underneath. He laid the grocery slip on the grass and watched it.

Inside the house, Reba squealed. "Oh! I saw a mouse. Or something."

"Don't harm him," Virgil called out to her; he heard her high heels clicking on the floor.

She came trotting out with a blue glass of water. "Didn't you get my letter?"

"Storm knocked over the mailbox. I haven't tended to it yet."

"Oh," she pouted. "It said everything. And it was on handmade paper Shirley Hope brought me from two or three oceans away. Or it was made a long time ago. I have trouble remembering these details since I've been gone. They told me to watch out for little slipups that would show I'm . . . not from around here," she said coyly.

"I may have received that letter," he said.

"Well?"

"I didn't read it, as it turned itself into a mouse. He's right around here. Spots."

"I can always laugh at your lies, Virgil. That cream-colored thing hiding in the kitchen?"

"Yes. That's your letter."

"That's your excuse. I've come back to you and the bargain's spelled out in the letter."

"That letter's gone past the reading of it. So you can forget about it. Or any bargains made only on your side."

"Maybe my letter hasn't come yet. What time's the mail around here?"

"Mail carrier won't leave any 'til he has a box set up for his use."

"I'll go get it from him myself." She poured the rest of the water on a lone, velvet snapdragon, the others all little wilted parcels, messages for another season.

"Reba, I heard you died out in Camus, Washington. Caught a chill. High fever."

"What fool told you that?"

"Glad you didn't die."

"I never was there. I did too die. I died in Chillicothe, Ohio. Poison."

"Hope it didn't pain you too much." Virgil smiled.

"No. Went out in a coma, wishing to . . . "

"What, sugar?"

"That if I was going to be dead . . . that you were dead too."

"Mail will be by shortly."

She got up, smoothed her dress and puffed her hair, picked her way to the end of the drive, met the mailman, and came back—lifting her skirt to hop the puddles—with a handful of mail.

"Don't you see? My being here is a miracle. I'm what you call Back From The Dead."

"Ah, Reba, I don't care you left and didn't let me know. I'm sufficiently glad you're back."

"I was dead. I am dead still. I can only stay if you're willing to admit I'm a miracle. If you believe I'm a miracle, then I am. If not, I'm gone."

"What woman hasn't asked for the same?"

"Oh, Virgil, if you can't be a little humble, I'll . . . have to go back."

"What's it like? Which one you take up residence in? Are you one of the good ones or the bad ones? Now I'll know," he chuckled.

"It's not like Sunday school," she explained. "It's confusing. They let me come back because I carried on so much for you. But they said you had to know for sure I'm a miracle or I can't stay. Oh, baby, don't you see?"

"You seem the same."

"Well, I am. Except for dead. I'm a miracle dead."

"Reba. Which is better: me believing you're a miracle from beyond the grave—which isn't exactly appetizing, girl—or you believing I just plain love you?"

Dust plumed a long way off. A car approached, turned down the path, and pulled up; the driver threw a canvas bag of mail at their feet, turned around, and careened out.

"Virgil. Why'd you let your mail pile up like this? You let yourself go, grieving for me?"

"No. I have no use for news."

"Well, I'm news. That's for sure." She squeezed herself around the middle.

"News is like a candle lit at noon. Candlelight shed on sunlight, no light at all," Virgil said with satisfaction. "Who else would get your news?"

"No one. That's the way the deal works. 'Cause if people knew, the system would fail or something. So, you're the only one. It's your miracle."

"None of those five thousand tattletales around." He lectured to Reba, "You know, from one gospel to the next the crowd increases a thousand fold, two loaves disappear, five more baskets of leftovers are gathered. That's gossip for you. That's the miracle of gossip, the past keeps getting grander, better or worse. Increased by a thousand fold and that doesn't even count women and children. They're not even counted. But they must have accounted for a good deal of the talebearing. Spreading the Word."

"But you're no Jesus. Neither am I. So there's to be no publicity."

"I hold no grudge, Reba. You didn't have to make up a tale to come back to me."

"You make me so mad sometimes, Virgil. I think I took off only to keep from killing you."

"I think you forget a lot."

She grabbed the hammer from the porch steps and swung at Virgil's temple.

"Now that makes more sense." He barely flinched.

"I could take you out and bring you back there with me, mister."

"That's right, Reba, if you were dead, wouldn't it stand to reason you'd want me to join you in eternity?" He plucked at dried weeds. "These were green not long ago. Or was it even hotter where you were? Do you suffer droughts, too, in the Hereafter? Hot? Were you in the hot place?" he teased.

"It was," she winked, "hot as sun-basking rocks, as bread browning in the oven, as a cock about to penetrate. Hot." She flung the hammer out of reach and curled up next to him; they tenderly felt each other's temperatures.

"Sounds like Heaven."

"No." She sat back. "There was litter all over the place—rotten animal corpses with little rotten corpses still in their shiny teeth. Leaves from gilt-edged books blowing all over—if you bent over to read one, you could hardly stop and the blood would rush to your head and your back would get a crick in it, but you couldn't stop reading until the pages ran out and then you'd fall over on top of them. The pages would melt beneath you and when you could get up again, you'd have this slime all over you, something like old spinach leaves but light colored and you could still see a few letters floating in it. And you'd still want to know. But you couldn't remember what you wanted to know."

"So you escaped from Hell?" He laughed and drew her down with him on top of suffering nasturtiums.

"No. What they say about the music is true. It's great."

"You'd better stay here with me, Reba," he whispered.

"I will. Soon's you say I'm a miracle."

"I will say no such thing."

"If you don't believe I'm a miracle, I can't stay," she cried. "Virgil, you're so contrary, you never believe anything against nature. There's not much time. The slightest thing ruins it. When I was crying over you, I just happened to say—and it certainly was true—that I had never got a chance to own one dress on earth that was fit to be buried in. They almost didn't let me come back to you, just for that. But I told them you loved me so much, just the sight of me'd make you say, 'It's a miracle.' So they figured it was worth it. For you." She got up and made little fists of frustration in her hair.

"So there it is. I have discovered, Reba, that miracles don't exist outside the telling of them. And you say your miracle endures only as a secret. I guess that's why we live in two different worlds." The mouse appeared and nibbled the grocery slip with Virgil's self-portrait. Virgil laughed like a cough. "Shit, Mouse, you're just a joke on me. But jokes might be like miracles, as they need to go somewhere, get around town and be with people to be of any use. Though a joke might be a good defense against too many miracles, huh, Mouse?"

Reba squealed again, seeing the mouse again. She jumped up and down on her high heels again.

"Reba. What you been through—whatever the address was—you can't act silly on seeing a mouse. It must not have been so tough there. Get that hammer, woman. I think I'll come on back with you. I'll never get to all the repairs this place needs and the drought—despite that storm—is hanging on. Did you cause that storm when you burst the boundaries between this world and the next?"

"You just don't know what I saw. When I was there. I saw two people aching for each other. They were trembling and weeping, just gazing into each other's eyes. One would shudder and then the other, seeing it, would shudder too."

"So, it was Heaven, after all. And there are rules." Virgil shook his head in mock disappointment.

"I did a terrible thing. And you'd think you're past sin once you're dead," she sighed. "I said it softly, 'Go ahead.' They heard me and reached for each other. But every place they touched, tongue to lip, hand to thigh, they stuck, glued. And whenever they tried to pull apart, their flesh tore and bled as though they were paper dolls and their sweat and blood was glue. They hurt so, but still they couldn't stop desiring. They tore each other to pieces, but they never stopped reaching for each other. Oh, Virgil, unless I can come back and love you now, the way it is here—"

"You about tore me up, Reba. You did just that."

"But I'm telling you. We've got a chance now."

"What'll I do? Wake up in the nights to find you're a goat or a dog or a fox in certain full moons. I think the strain might be too much."

Reba pranced back into the house. "I'm done talking to you."

Virgil got up and put away the hammer. Noticing the paint cans, he painted the doghouse sky blue with a border of tulips and cracked hearts, thinking a dog or some other animal would show up one day soon. When he cleaned up and went into the house, he searched over and over, like running a maze, but Reba was gone. Wind burst into the house, swirling and searching with him.

"She should have gathered up all this mail I'm not about to open. Dragged as it was—and stuffed with messages—from the other side." The wind subsided and died an empty promise.

The mouse darted among parched snapdragons and scattered letters until the night faded, when in the new sun it became an envelope again.

=◇=

Strawberry Maiden, All Day on a Chain

THAT BASEMENT HAS more than fruit jars and a sled. The cement's always damp from the blood. And there are always little whoosh sounds from the dancing.

We know, we snuck down there maybe a thousand times. Three times this summer. All we do is push that window open at the top, then, Kimmie says, make ourselves in the shape of a piece of pie to fit through the space, then climb down the shelves with all the old jars chattering their teeth. It makes your heart beat like crazy.

The neighbors watch the place so hard and pretend so hard not to see. The house looks like all the others on the road. These are bungalows, Kimmie's dad says. I asked my dad, he says they are mortgages.

Rachel Ryan's house, except that it's overtop that basement, is almost just exactly like mine and Kimmie's. It has plain white boards all over it, plain bushes all around it, and plain chairs and beds all inside it. A couple times we went into the house itself while Rachel Ryan went off for about ten hours, forgetting to hook the back screen door. Mom told Dad, that woman's got nothing better to do than sit in the library reading books, with no kids and now him gone, just her five shades of lipstick and twenty pairs of shoes to keep her busy.

Three pairs of shoes, one lipstick. Well, there were two lipsticks, but Kimmie got one. Nothing else. Mom just made that up, I guess, thinking no one would ever be brave enough to go get the whole truth. There's nothing in Rachel Ryan's house that's interesting. Except for a couple of jello molds hanging on the kitchen wall, a lobster and a heart. Kimmie had to keep from laughing. Imagine Rachel Ryan making him jiggly lobsters for dinner. And hearts full of fruit cocktail. Maybe the mirror with painted peacocks is pretty interesting. Whoever looks in gets those long-tailed chickens sitting in their hair and pecking at their necks. We stood on the dictionary and a cushion to be tall as Rachel Ryan looking in the mirror. Whenever Rachel Ryan looks in that mirror to check and see if she lost her mind, she finds those peacocks roosting there.

Everyone says she had been locked down there in the basement for twenty-five years, only let loose to dance, until she agreed. How could something like that have happened so close by? All the houses are alike up and down the road. Mrs. Brooks is proud to say, You can pick mine out, it's the only one on the road with venetian blinds. The paint's always peeling on Eli and Sweetie's house. Ours has Fanny out front, sleeping or barking. And Kimmie's house has a For Sale sign her parents pound into the grass each summer, just in case. When we were real little, we used the sign for the ally-ally-outs-in-free.

So Kimmie and I don't have much to look at except the dances that used to happen out in the dark, up out of that basement, and onto the deserted strawberry field behind our little houses. Foreclosed. The bank foreclosed the strawberries so we get them free and Eli and Sweetie don't get them at all. Even though they used to make the field even as pleats and sell the berries in little wooden cups. I can remember the pleats.

And the cups we got down in Rachel Ryan's basement. Mom thought Sweetie gave them to us, says they used to have the balsawood ones long, long ago, twelve baskets to a flat. A flat was this slatted wooden crate, they filled up right in the strawberry field. Now we just take a bowl out and get what we want. Mostly they rot. A long time ago we used to have one of those wooden crates with a handle in the middle for Fanny's water dish on one side and her food dish on the other. She chewed it to pieces. Our little baskets are spotted with strawberry juice and some with blood. Kimmie and I keep them down in our basement. We keep the lipstick in one, our ten-dollar bill we found in Rachel Ryan's drawer in another. It was really about the only thing we saw in her house that had belonged to him. She must have burned all the rest of his stuff. We got a spoonful of the ashes from out back and put them in gum-wrapper silver, in the fifth basket. We keep a whole row of those little wooden baskets with the pieces we gather in them. Down in our plain old basement with no blood, no secret dancing, no chains, no wax. Except we scraped up a blob of wax from Rachel Ryan's basement that had dripped from one of the sealed promises and put it in one of the wooden cups.

That was a courtship unlike any since Adam & Eve, my mom says when she forgets I'm around to hear it. Yeah, my dad said once. But the marriage turned out the same, anyway. We got meat loaf for three days.

It would make you wonder, wouldn't it, why those basement steps are the only ones made of stone? Our steps are climb-through wooden ones. And it's true, down there in Rachel Ryan's basement are scratches on the wall like a prisoner's calendar. And it's true there is an iron ring in the floor, right where the drain is. And it's true that there are blobs of wax dripped from the wax seals stuck on the promises Rachel Ryan was made to sign. Some of our own candle wax splattered there, too.

She looks pretty for someone held hostage in a dungeon for twenty-five years. She always has to wear long sleeves, though, so we can't even see where the handcuffs made marks that can never go away and where her skin always scraped against the damp basement all those years. She has been wounded, Mrs. Brooks says, but you can't see anything except some tiny cracks down her cheeks. One time we were down in that basement, Kimmie even found a little shred of skin stuck to the wall. We've got it. I didn't touch it, only Kimmie.

Our mom lets us have our playhouse under the stairs, she calls it, and says my brother has to leave us alone. He says he likes Fanny better than us, anyway. Mom doesn't come down much except to scrub with something she says is to keep mold and slime from crawling up the stairs at us. Kimmie says Rachel Ryan used to crawl up her stone-cold steps as far as her chains would go, then fall back, every time. Scrape herself up. Kimmie and I go up our wooden steps hanging on from the back like monkey bars, our legs dangling over the boxes of Christmas decorations and the magazines of Dad's house plans. Then at the top, we hook our legs up, crawl through the space under the top stair, and roll over the ledge onto the kitchen floor. No matter how much they might yell to hurry for supper or go get Fanny or my brother, it's the rule. No stepping on the tops of the steps, only climbing from the backs of them.

I wonder how many times she was forced to mark Xs on his wax-sealed lies? I used to feel sorry for her, but Kimmie knows for a fact that once after Rachel Ryan was left off the chain to dance, he forgot to tie her up for the rest of the night when he threw her back down there. She could have climbed up the fruit-jar shelves, made herself into a slice of pie, and escaped through the hinged basement window. Later than midnight. It was always at midnight she danced. But not every night.

Kimmie says that was when Rachel Ryan went sort of nuts. The night when he forgot to lock her. She was about to climb up and slip through the window when she thought she had to find the others. She got it in her head that there were more slaves down there someplace and she had to find them and help them get away. She looked for them in the pitch dark, all night long, feeling along the bloody cement and moldy cracks. Rachel Ryan looked every place, like a blind person, even opening a jar of beans and sticking her hands in, her fingers thin as the string beans. Kimmie took down one of the jars and dared me to stick my hand in, saying there might be a finger in there. I knew there wasn't because there weren't really any other slaves kept in the basement, they were only Rachel Ryan's imaginary company. And because Rachel Ryan has every single finger you'd expect on anybody. I just didn't want to put my hand in old green beans. Kimmie couldn't get it open, but kept saying double-dare, anyway.

Mom doesn't always know the truth, either. She told Dad that Rachel Ryan could have left here a long time ago, but she just always

turned back, looking to pack her earrings. I'd like to tell Mom that the
only earrings we found in the velvet box on Rachel Ryan's dresser were
some little blue round ones and some gold squiggles. Nothing you'd
ever run back in a devil's house to get. Kimmie doesn't think it's worth
it to go get a set of them to put in our wooden strawberry boxes. She
wouldn't be too afraid to, though. And neither would I. Instead we got
a set of Kimmie's mother's earrings that are very beautiful with jewels.
We keep them like they were Rachel Ryan's.

What I truly wish we could get are two of the stains. One bloodstain is like a picture of her when she first got tied up. You can see how
really beautiful she was. The other bloodstain is of her dancing.
Whoosh. Whoosh. Whoosh. My little brother always goes around
saying whoosh just because he's heard us. It sounds stupid because he
doesn't really understand.

Maybe it's okay after all to live all day on a chain if you get let off it
sometimes to dance across the strawberries. Mom doesn't have a chain,
but when did she ever dance? But even Rachel Ryan doesn't dance out
there anymore, now that he's not there to make her. Kimmie and I always watch at midnight whenever we stay overnight at each other's
house, just to make sure. Sometimes you can almost see her, but what
you can see is leftover whooshes from the old dances, not her out
there now.

Kimmie's mom said, after twenty-five years when Rachel Ryan
started liking him and acting like a regular wife, he just didn't want to
stay. My mom said, if she hadn't acted like a fool whenever he let her
loose, you could almost just cry for her. Sweetie said, Rachel Ryan has
already done her time in Hell, so she can do whatever she wants to with
the time she's got left on earth. Mrs. Brooks said she only wishes she
had got a good look at him, only ever really knowing the prisoner. But
she's pretty sure she's seen him coming by sometimes, really slow,
looking at everything. Kimmie heard Mrs. Brooks tell her mother that
Rachel Ryan was his love slave.

Kimmie and I act her out sometimes. We dance in the whooshes
until we fall down and get squashed strawberry spots. Then I whisper,

run, run, run. I cannot go, Rachel Ryan gasps—really Kimmie—I cannot find my earrings. She used to say, I cannot find the others. The
prisoners. But she likes this better. I probably shouldn't have let what
mom said get mixed up in the truth.

Once both our moms yelled at us, both at the same time, to stop
wrecking the strawberries. They are foreclosed strawberries, what can
it matter? Eli and Sweetie won't go near them. They are lost, every last
berry, says Sweetie, even though she can see them out her kitchen win-

dow. Both moms were screaming at us, but we couldn't figure out how to get up because we were laughing and because Rachel Ryan was totally drained away from her dancing. I cannot go, Rachel Ryan Kimmie whispered, I cannot find my ears. She meant earrings. But we laughed so hard she whispered, I cannot go, I cannot find my hands. I cannot go, I cannot find my feet, I danced them off. We laughed until we really almost lost our own selves.

=◇=

Of All God's Creatures

The CHILDREN WENT to the attic and found a picnic basket. Drawing back the embroidered cloth, they came upon a coiled gift.

Although they had not expected the snake, it was an expectant snake, with a distension in its sinewy form like a large loaf of bread and now and then like a sailing ship. The snake told them it had been waiting millennia in the picnic basket: a serpent in waiting. The child, or whatever it was, was not due for years to come.

The snake was a sweet companion and went everywhere with them. At the theatre she coiled into both laps at once, and in the scary parts slid up under their shorts and shirts, wrapping around their necks; then cheek to cheek to cheek they laughed and wept at the spectacles. They played crack-the-whip except when the snake had morning sickness; then they played hide-the-thimble, which the snake always won. They played a pebble game they drew in the dirt from the snake's old memory; and the snake, when she was losing, would get so excited she'd swallow her stone markers. The children yearned for the snake's baby; they didn't know why, they were expecting nothing. They would lie around together in the long afternoons and tell one another stories, or gaze at the protrusion in the snake's long, graceful body. They played hide-and-seek, squealing when she'd snake up on them.

When will it be born? they asked as they stroked the bulge. The snake calculated for a long time, having to try again and again. The snake had no fingers on which to count and the children felt sorry. Would you rather, they asked each other, be the most beautiful of all god's creatures or have fingers to help you do sums and ciphers? That question was once put to me, the snake flickered. Of course, right now

I don't look my best, she said, passing in front of the mirror. I'll get my old figure back one of these days, when the little bundle arrives. They traced the shadows of her silhouette, and by that method learned to draw. It seemed, when they felt around the edges, to be a little car or perhaps a deer, even a human child. Your child will have legs, they speculated shyly.

She watched the children play dress-up with feather boas, velvet vests, fig leaves, old satin high heels. You look cleverer all naked, the snake observed cunningly. They offered to dress the snake, but she had nothing in her den but old striped suspenders. They petted her and put their ears next to her swelling. Yes, but when will it be born? The snake coiled around them, telling them again how happy they'd all be together, close. She squeezed them and tickled. When? they giggled and gasped for breath. She tried to calculate her time again, winding back and forth over a length of her own mosaic. Without fingers, one has to make do without numbers, said the snake. Well? It won't be long now, grinned the snake, extending herself into a single straight line. Watch, she said. And then she suddenly swallowed her tail and circled the garden. Remember these poses and you don't need fingers. And she did them again: a singular stretch and then a hurrying circle.

She gave them a new idea, telling them the secret of their own disappearance. Then, they protested, by the time your baby comes we'll be too old to play with it if what you say is true, that we won't be children forever. She turned a future when they would get big while waiting for her to shrink, when she would eject from her flesh the child of their own childhood's desire, the infant of the snake. So the snake performed a shadow play for them, a drama of their encroaching mortality.

They looked closer, ran their hands along the beaded ridge of the snake. What would it be? I think, said one, it's a fairy baby; I think, responded the other, it's a rhinoceros baby. Of one thing they were sure: the child did not resemble the mother. There was no snake in the snake. The serpent dripped from the trees and ignored them. Leave me to my longing, she said.

Much as they loved her, they desired what was in her but did not resemble her. The serpent slid back to them, content to play dolls or soccer—turning her leftover flesh into cradles or supple boundary lines.

As the snake smelled them with her pink and pointed tongue, giving them double and double-quick kisses, they modeled an alphabet from the forks and flickers. They wrote stories for her baby to read. They made a city for it, because the snake asked them to consider that they might not be home when it finally arrived.

And since they had come to investigate, to name and to ornament the world, they came to want a baby, too. To emulate the snake's mystery? Or to ensure that some old memory of themselves would be around when she at last couched for birth? They tried with their sums and ciphers, they tried with their alphabets and the pebble game they played in the dust. Can't get the hang of it? the snake snickered and looped herself from a branch, making a swing for them.

All went well until her belly seemed to deflate. When the children worried and cried, she swallowed them up. Have a look inside, she said, and slithered around the garden out back, humming, as though the children were the child she expected. How surprised they'll be, she said, to see how we get with children; how surprised they'll be, wound close inside me in the dark, to learn they are to be my most mysterious serpent infants, the object of my expectations.

=⟩=

Seven Deadly Skins

Eager and awkward, that dog might have come up overnight from the Devil Himself. A creature formed by haste and faulty memory, the teacher observed as she shooed him away from the schoolyard. Some dog, the fidgety grocer's son grinned, sneaking out the heel of bologna to him.

The grocer's son was the prettiest thing in town; so handsome he quickened the pulse of commerce. Girls offered to go to the store for their mommas. And, when her daughter mentioned the store, a momma might suddenly realize she was coming to the end of the baking powder. She'd find a spatter down her front, a reason to change, run a comb through her hair, and fly to the store. Some mommas brought their daughters along; some made them stay home to watch the soup or the baby. The girls wheedled their daddies for coins. Dads handed over coins to their daughters, speculating on their futures.

Gloria needed, she said, a barrette. For the sake of mathematics, Gloria said. If I could keep my hair out of my eyes, I could learn how to do the problems. That's what the teacher said. When her daddy heard her mention the store, he, like other daddies in town, recalled the eligibility of the grocer's son. Gloria went shopping.

Legs longer than his back, the stray dog was standing out by the mailbox, and trotted along with Gloria to the store. The grocer's son stepped out on the porch and rubbed the dog's ragged ears.

The barrettes lay on cotton batting, right at the front of the display case by the cash register, in front of the ammunition, the pocketknives, and penny candy. Gloria pondered shiny blue streaks, a cherub, a parrot, and settled on the red rose. The grocer's son winked at her when he handed over the ten cents in change. She went home and her dad called her his pride and joy.

Gloria wore the rose barrette to school. Along every row of desks, girls bent over books holding back their silky hair with barrettes—swans, kissing bluebirds, golden shoes. Investments in barrettes led to the inventions of fashion. Neva Jean came to school one day with three barrettes sprayed over her right ear—blue tulips, yellow duck, silver moon—and four arched over the left—fox, clasped ivory hands, fan, metallic bowtie. The other girls felt shy, almost naked. Gloria was quiet, her hands flitted through her hair.

The grocer's son opened a flimsy cardboard box and put out some new barrettes in the little glass showcase: Scotties, a miniature hand mirror with real glass, tortoiseshell hearts, a pencil and a pen, a peacock. He checked the cans of bait in the cooler. The grizzled dog came whining to the screen door, tall enough to look overtop the Skoal sign. The grocer's son cut off a hard corner of cheddar, tossing it out on the porch. He turned the radio up loud, yearning for whatever wasn't shelved or cellophaned.

The tattered dog followed after Mr. S. H. Rehmur, new himself to town, settling in for months before anyone knew or tried his first name. His hair waved down over his collar and as soon as he got that missing tooth pegged, there were women who were cooking and dieting, getting ready. Folks in this town would pop their seams if they got all they craved, Mr. S. H. Rehmur told the grocer's son as he ordered his sardines, crackers, and bait. Fish this time of year would bite at one of them hair claps, he gestured toward the display. Every one just an empty belly, an open mouth. The grocer's son watched the panting dog unfurl his voluminous tongue. My dog likes you, S. H. Rehmur noted. Tell you what, for these sardines and fishworms, I'll trade. Sure, said the grocer's son, but I thought he was a stray. Throw in some shotgun shells, he's yours. Okay. And maybe a sack of flour. The grocer's son shrugged, may as well. And may as well add in a box of matches, S. H. Rehmur said and whistled the dog right into the store. Don't stint and the dog will be obliged; a side of bacon and a pint of that whiskey you got in the back there and a handful of chocolate bars will do. The grocer's son gathered the supplies. Better hand over that little red-apple hair clap. I'll put it on my line and bring you the fish it catches. He left with a carton balanced on one shoulder, a sack of flour on the other. The grocer's son opened a can of potted meat for the dog and tossed malted milk balls in the air for both of them to catch in their mouths. The bell jangled on the door as the dog pushed it open and loped after S. H. Rehmur's Oldsmobile.

Gloria asked her daddy for money for a barrette. He recalled she had a new barrette and thought a girl ought not be too sassy. She sighed and explained to him, it seems only one side of her face was able to see the numbers in the book, she needed both eyes. Money tree didn't bloom yet, he said, though S. H. Rehmur says he may have something here pretty soon. Neva Jean wears seven or eight at once, Gloria told him. Our hen didn't lay the golden egg yet, Momma told Gloria, handing her Baby Donny, all sticky. And Momma, always thin-skinned, said she didn't want S. H. Rehmur looking down on them, he himself missing a big front tooth.

Big brother Seth found out S. H. Rehmur owned hotels in places like Memphis and Honolulu. Seth holed up in his room, waiting for opportunity to knock. Momma said, I don't know if that boy's a mouse or a bat, but he won't show his face in the sunshine. Gloria turned her back on the weathered house that shamed her. Just under the upstairs window parallel to her own was a stain that deepened every day, as though the house had a weepy sty in its left eye. Momma was sure the house was too close to the river, causing moisture to spot the siding. And she got mad again that the catywampus house didn't look anything like the picture of a house she was promised. Gloria knew the wet spot was from Seth relieving himself out the window to save from having to leave his room. He gave Gloria his loose change to keep her from pestering him.

She went to the store. She got the hand-mirror barrette. The grocer's son said, try it on here, why don'tcha? The big dog jumped up and put his paws on her shoulders. But when she got home, Gloria's mother narrowed her eyes at the lady's mirror and said, put the potatoes on to boil. Don't cut so careless you throw the potato half away.

Mr. S. H. Rehmur came in, looked in the oven, the icebox, and the sink, remarking that her mother could pare so thin, it could be gold leaf. Her mother didn't set him right. Mr. Rehmur showed them his missing tooth. First he showed it missing in his smile, then showed the tooth he carried in his vest pocket. Gloria's mother laughed like shattering glass. Gloria took Baby Donny outside. They watched the dog roll on his back in the road, then patted the dust out of his matted coat. S. H. Rehmur washed up for supper.

Gloria wore the little vanity mirror in her hair. During the math lesson the teacher demanded, what's all this commotion? Two boys had discovered a little dancing circle of light on the ceiling. Everyone pointed. Even the teacher was perplexed, though she disputed it was a fairy or God himself, letting the class know, furthermore, neither topic was fit for class. Gloria couldn't see the miraculous light that had come to school and appeared to everyone else. Whenever she looked in the direction the class pointed, the light jumped to another part of the room. It might be God after all, she thought, and I'm missing him. I can't see it, she cried. The teacher stared at her, then walked right back to Gloria's desk. Look, class, I have solved this mystery. Use your heads. And Gloria, you hold your head still. The teacher laid her hand on the side of Gloria's head and the little light vanished. She took her hand away and the light popped back onto the ceiling. The teacher was disappointed in a class that hadn't applied the principles of reflection. I'm afraid I'll have to keep this hairclasp. She undid it from Gloria's hair and said she was disappointed especially in Gloria, for causing such an uproar. She put the little mirror in her desk drawer, and that's where it will stay. And Gloria, you will stay after and do another page of problems.

The teacher said it was time to think of others, and everyone should bring in a can of food for the unfortunate. Neva Jean bragged she could bring in Spanish olives. Each day, the teacher would hold up mincemeat, pears, baked beans, fruit cocktail, and praise the donors, giving lessons on nutrition and agriculture as well as charity. If you can't spare, it's all right, said the teacher and Gloria let her hair fall over her face like a curtain.

Momma, she said again, I need just one can of food for the unfortunate. Her dad was patient, we just get by, Glory, by the skin of our teeth. Should change soon, though. Gloria went to the store again, examining the canned goods. What'll it be? asked the grocer's son. You just looking? he asked, thinking he was the canned ham. I'll be back, she said. Your old dog's just skin and bones, she flirted with the grocer's son. He cracked an egg, and they watched the dog lick it out, the membrane from the shell stuck like a little note pinned to his nose.

Momma frowned, one more mouth as it is, don't you see? How can you be so silly about a can of food? You're just letting your pride outrace your sense. Grandma moving in meant Baby Donny was in Gloria's room, but she didn't mind all that much. Grandma was hauled in with some fine things and Gloria could spy herself in every one of them. Inclined to glimpse her cheek in the bowl of the serving spoon, to test the flight of her hand in the mahogany veneer of the buffet, even her foot reflected in the brass pedestal of the floor lamp, Gloria found Grandma's arrival was not all bad. Though Seth found the air in the house even more close and on clear nights slept on the porch. That dog curled up there with him.

It's winter coming on, Momma reminded him. Come in off the front porch. I hope you don't think we're going to feed a dog too, and reminded Seth it was time he got to that carburetor. Grandma had sharp eyesight and intended to straighten things out. When Seth stuck his finger in the pan of Donny's milk, Grandma saw the film cling to it, and said, boy, that's how you'll turn out, scum, neither flesh nor spirit. Seth poured out the milk and drank it in one gulp. Well, said Dad, it's the most appetite I've seen him get for awhile. Seth lugged Grandma back to her bed.

The grocer came into town once a month to count the money. Coins beget coins, he said, be mindful of every one. The grocer's son and the long-legged dog watched. Gloria came in to read the labels again. Don't handle the merchandise if you don't intend to take it home, said the skinflint grocer. He went to hide the money in the back room, and the dog followed him. Not even the grocer's son was allowed to see the secret place, and never found it when he searched. Leave the money be, the grocer had told him. Money is like folks, put enough together in a dark spot and always makes more. The grocer's son laughed. He looked at Gloria and said a man could starve to death before she'd make up her mind to buy a crust of bread. Where'd that dog come from? the grocer asked. It's hers, said the grocer's son. Gloria ran all the way home, the dog catching up with her and running around and around her.

Here, momma said, take this oatmeal up to the old glutton. Watered-down oatmeal is all grandma eats, said Gloria. That's because she want to live forever, the greedy old thing.

Evaporated milk, cherry jam, corned beef—even the boys remembered to bring their donations to school—Campbell's soup, baking powder, cocoa. The teacher said cocoa grew on trees in South America and even a box of salt would go a long way to help the unfortunate. Neva Jean arranged the cans, decking them with paper chains and stickery holly leaves. She kept track in her head and reminded those who had not yet brought their charity. The teacher gave the unfortunate a cake of Ivory soap and the class a talk on hygiene.

On the way home, Gloria saw Mr. S. H. Rehmur beside the road. He said, you need some money. I need, she said, thick-cut marmalade from England, in a handsome stone jar. What would you do for it? Would you sit up on the hood of my Oldsmobile and let this old dog lick your knees? Gloria climbed up the chrome and the ragged-eared dog, as though he knew his part, licked her smooth knee and then the one she skinned up on Baby Donny's iron bed. Mr. S. H. Rehmur hunched on the curb, writing in a little notebook with the stub of a pencil. After an hour, S. H. Rehmur counted out the coins. He and Gloria both knew the price of marmalade to the penny.

When she got to the store, the grocer's son looked at her. You got something nice, he said, handing over the marmalade. He gave her a Coca-Cola, the tall dog a bit of pork rind, and invited Gloria to sit up on the counter with him.

Where you been? her momma complained. Take the baby. Been talking to the grocer's son again, her dad guessed from his chair by the stove. Beauty is only skin deep, crinkled Grandma observed. Gloria didn't mind setting the table, not since the dining-room set had been delivered along with Grandma.

Gloria hid the marmalade under her pillow and later looked at it in the moonlight, wishing she and Baby Donny could have one spoonful each, without breaking the seal. Maybe a half-teaspoon of it in Grandma's oatmeal, and maybe not. We sat on the countertop, both of us, she told Baby Donny in the night. Drinking Cokes together. Maybe I have a boyfriend, she whispered to the baby, and maybe for sure I have the most beautiful canned food for the unfortunate.

At school, Gloria handed over the stone jar of marmalade with its significant stickers and fine lettering, and waited for the praise. The teacher gave a lesson of how marmalade was invented after a shipload of Spanish oranges got spoiled by seawater on their way to England. The class laughed. The teacher, with a lesson on geography and enter-prise, told how the women chopped up the worthless orange rinds and cooked them in honey and then all the Englishmen started to spread this new preserve on their biscuits. The class laughed again and the teacher let them, as it was the day before holiday. And furthermore, Englishmen, the schoolteacher said, call their cookies by the name of biscuits and call their biscuits by the name of buns. The class laughed and Neva Jean asked right out loud, Gloria, where'd you ever come up with such an odd gift for the unfortunate? I myself have given some-thing they could never taste in ten years, Spanish olives. In addition to

a cake of Ivory soap, I am donating this green tea, which is all the way from the land of China, said the schoolteacher, settling the matter.

Mr. S. H. Rehmur came to the classroom and the biggest boys helped carry the provisions out to his Oldsmobile. So busy shaking hands and blushing and saying she hoped he had a chance for some good cooking over the holidays, the teacher didn't even seem to notice the big dog walking right into the classroom and helping himself to the

iced gingerbread man Neva Jean had brought her. Mr. S. H. Rehmur
stuck the tip of his tongue through the space in his teeth and looked
over the class.

I know for sure one thing I'll get under the tree, Neva Jean told the
girls on the way home from school. Mittens made with rabbit fur. My
daddy saw the softest pelts Mr. S. H. Rehmur had and just knew I
ought to have them. I heard him tell my momma, that man drives a
trade, but they're for Neva Jean. Another of the girls said, I'm sure to
get about ten barrettes. Barrettes are for children, said Neva Jean, tossing her hair. And, my daddy's thinking he'll soon let me invite someone to Sunday pie.

You're too young for boyfriends yet, Gloria's mother talked non-
stop, polish up the dining-room suit, your father's offered it to S. H.
Rehmur to get us by, as he admired it when he was here for supper,
your brother Seth is down with a mean cough, take this oatmeal up to
Grandma, she has to be fed with a spoon these days, and get the baby
out of my hair, and don't carry on about a few sticks of furniture, when
we get back on our feet, S. H. Rehmur's going to let us buy it back,
same price, he promised Grandma. As she tried to poke oatmeal in her,
Gloria told Grandma, I think the grocer's son likes me enough to give
me a Coca-Cola and ask me to sit up on the counter with him.
Grandma told her about a fish washed up out of the river had a girl's
hair-bow in its gut. Then she fed the leftover oatmeal to Baby Donny
and told him again about her having a drink of pop with the grocer's
son. It's hard to know what babies and grandmas can understand.

On Christmas Eve, Gloria looked out the window and saw the
grocer's delivery truck coming down the road. He's coming to see me.
She ran to look in the glass, to comb her hair, to put in her red-rose
barrette, then take it out and put it back in the drawer of Grandma's
buffet. S. H. Rehmur wouldn't pick up his dining-room set until after
the New Year. Her dad looked down the road and said, Glory, he
wants to invite you to take a ride in the delivery truck. I'll carry
Grandma downstairs to meet him. Get Seth out of bed and we'll have

coffee at the dining-room table, her mother demanded. She yanked Baby Donny's washing, not quite dry, from the line over the stove. Everyone peeped out the windows as the grocer's son pulled into the yard and hefted a big box out the back of the pickup. The long-legged dog jumped down and ran around to the back door. Both the box and the dog had been done up with fine red bows. The grocer's son, too, avoided the front door and went around to the back porch. He left the box on the step and drove off without ever knocking.

Gloria's dad, still out of breath from packing Grandma downstairs, brought the box in and set it on the kitchen table. I'll be, I just don't know what this could be, weighs more than Grandma. Don't let that mangy dog in here, her mother said. The dog, spit-drizzling tongue, padded into the kitchen. Pack me in there, Grandma called from the other room. Seth set her up beside the box. She observed, that's the kind of suitor to have, one with a store. There's a card. Too shy to come in and sit with us, her dad said, but a good fellow. Read the card. A box of canned goods for a sweetheart instead of a pearl necklace? Seth asked.

Gloria tripped on the scatter rug, knocking the calendar off the wall. Her dad handed her the card. Read it to us, Glory. If it's not too mushy, her grandma added. Momma snatched the hand-lettered card from her and read out in a tight voice, For the Unfortunate this Holiday Season. With all best wishes for a prosperous New Year. your Neighbors.

Seth pulled cocoa and chicken soup from the box. The turkey, wrapped in butcher paper and tied with string, was discreetly tagged, Special Order, S H R. Grandma said, I think I see canned peaches there, too. Seth and Gloria's dad put everything out on the table. No one made mention of the stone jar of English, thick-cut marmalade.

Gloria's dad said it was a mystery to him why these provisions would be delivered to this house, just when there's coming a turn for the better. Seth said he was likely to get back at the grocer's son for this. Grandma said it looked like she had been moved right into a nest of disgrace. But I could eat peaches, that's one thing. Gloria's dad said, here's what happened: the grocer's son come by to see Gloria and took her this fine Christmas present to her family. But he also had to take some goods to some folks who weren't doing so well. The card to those folks dropped by accident into this box. They all followed Momma out of the kitchen, leaving Grandma to holler at the decorated dog, who took the turkey by the knotted string and ran off with it, leaving the back door open and icy wind blowing into the kitchen.

Someone broke into the store. Grandma leaned like a rag doll wherever anyone propped her in the house, but she had more news than a radio, giving out the latest on the whole town. Got off with a bag of money, she reported. And every single Hershey bar. Neva Jean was seen walking down the street and the grocer's son holding onto her hand or anyway holding on to her by her new rabbit-hair mittens. And it's been said the teacher might not be an old maid after all. My dining-room set is nowhere in town, handed over to an auction house, gone for good. That old crooked-legged dog showed up at the school with a bloody rabbit in its mouth, but turned out to be a pair of mittens. Both left and right.

The grocer questioned his own son. Maybe, said the grocer's son, if you had ever shown me where it was, I could have watched out for it, but you never let anyone know where you hide the money except that dog. Why don't you ask him? The dog was sleeping next to the egg crates and the grocer kicked him. Mr. S. H. Rehmur came in looking for an apple to bring to the schoolteacher. He offered to take the dog off his hands. For a few dollars I'll see to it he doesn't come around. The grocer gave him two dollar bills. Mr. S. H. Rehmur added them to a neat bundle held with a thick rubber band, just the kind the grocer used to bundle his own money. Better let me have some shells to put him out of his misery and a hunk of bologna for his last meal, he's been a good old pup. The grocer nodded. Maybe a box of rat poison, too, in case I miss my shot. Too bad you run out of apples. The grocer got down the rat poison.

Mr. S. H. Rehmur brought the teacher applesauce. Mr. S. H. Rehmur's Oldsmobile was seen out in front of the teacher's house again, Grandma announced. And he brought the teacher a dog, and she thought she'd learn to like the dog when S. H. Rehmur told her there's no end of suffering in this town. The teacher agreed, telling him she could see beneath the surface of things. He told her there are those who would rather poison a dog than give him a fried egg every Friday, which is all in this world he wants. The teacher said she'd be glad to have someone to cook for, even if it was only a fried egg once a week when school was out.

I wasn't even surprised, Grandma said, when that man moved right in with her. Didn't surprise me a bit when she took sick and left us before Easter. But it sure took me by surprise that S. H. Rehmur turned out to take up her class, I never would have guessed him for a scholar.

Gloria said, you can't make me go to school anymore. He's got Neva Jean sitting in a chair right beside him and marking everybody's tests with the teacher's own red pencil. She doesn't even mind using a dead teacher's pencil. He found my mirror hair barrette in the teacher's desk and gave it to Neva Jean. I'm not going back. Her momma answered, don't carry on, you wanted to quit school even before the teacher died, and you've been saying you won't go to the store ever again, and you refuse to set the table anymore, now that you lost your dining suit. You let everything get under your skin, Glory, and just tire me out.

Maybe she is dead same as the teacher, Grandma considered when Neva Jean disappeared. Though I heard she just run off. The school shut down again while everyone dragged the river. But, Grandma whispered, let me tell you what I heard. When S. H. Rehmur gets back he means to come courting Gloria. She might could get back my mahogany dining-room set. Then she could quit school if she took a notion, having a teacher right by her side. Anyway, he's only teaching school long enough for her class to pass, just out of the goodness of his heart. Too bad Mr. S. H. Rehmur was called away, he could advise the search party. But he'll surely be back before his class needs their final grades. And he'll be back for our girl. Gloria wouldn't be advised to go throwing herself at the grocer's son again, he's got no sense. Every day that fool hangs link sausages out in front of the store trying to entice that ugly dog to come back to him.

This Is How We Got to Be Three Pods and a Pea

I'VE GOT THREE AUNTS and no mom. Not a breath of a dad and no uncles. One grandaddy who says I've got too many aunts. Grandaddy says he was cursed with all these females. That's counting me, too.

The aunts all agree to the date. It was sixteen years ago. Before me. He was saying his grace every night at supper, and the aunts all agree down to the letter that he prayed, Lord, too many girls, get a man for at least one of them or pack me to Heaven, where there's sure to be lots of men and not hardly a woman. Except when my aunts cried, he allowed that their momma is one female who must surely be in Heaven. His wife. My Grandma Fernie. I only get to see her in pictures Aunt Tish shows me, looking younger than my aunts look now. We were young like you then, they tell me. So young it could hurt their feelings, as they had to listen to him grumble about all these girls, even as one was missing from the table, their mom, her empty chair almost still warm. Aunt Fern says I sit in her chair. Aunt Celie says that I'm just lucky not ever to have had a mom, because when she's dead and gone it's sadder than a naked bird.

He complained, they tell me, about the aunts' roast beef and pies. Even the peas weren't as good as Grandma Fernie had made. They still cried all the time for her, they say, hating to hear Grandaddy complain to God about Grandma Fernie in Heaven and not in the kitchen, where his girls were so bad they burned water. So that was the year they tricked him. He's been so mad ever since that he gave up, Aunt Tish says, praying for his virile heaven and has, he always says, to suffer in a house with not one plumb wall and clotted up with all these old girls. Can't blame him completely. Except that he says the one young one's turning out the same. But I'm not.

My aunt Tish sees me painting the cat's fingernails and sits down with me on the rug and says it was really my Aunt Celie's doing. She means when Aunt Celie ran off, got as far as Deer Lodge, Montana, and the fanbelt popped. A prison town. There she was, a saggy old silk scarf holding back her in-a-hurry hair, in her jeans she'd put on and sit down in a tub of water, just so when they were dry, you'd know exactly who was inside them. She poked every record and nail polish she ever owned into the Falcon, plus all the mascaras and shadows belonging to Aunt Tish and Aunt Fern, plus all their sweaters and storybooks. Then Celie and the Falcon ran to a sweat across the hot summer.

Aunt Fern remembers it, too, and tells me, it served her right, Celie stole my angora sweater and Grandaddy's station wagon right out from under our noses. It served her right to break down right in a prison town. It was a sign. That car's fanbelt dropped her right where she belonged. In jail almost.

Aunt Celie saw it as a sign, too, but on her side of things. It was so hot Celie had to make herself a shirt out of Grandma Fernie's hankies, the only pretty things left me, says Aunt Fern, aside from Grandma Fernie's own frilly name.

That's one female down, Grandaddy must have thought. He must have prayed her away, and he was thinking he could get rid of the lot of them by prayers if not by marriage, Aunt Tish says.

Aunt Celie showed me how to make a hanky shirt once. Forty-five seconds in a real emergency, she says. I don't know what kind of emergency.

Even though the mechanic told Celie to stay where it was cool, she walked around the hot town of Deer Lodge so she wouldn't have to sit and smell the oil, look at how sad that Ford was, and hear again and again how it was the damnedest thing, every size belt hanging there but the one you need, it never fails. I can almost see them myself, says Aunt Tish, those imperfect bands of infinity, hanging on nails in the dank garage. Celie called the car the Falcon, never the station wagon, as Aunt Celie never likes to humiliate anyone, especially not a car that tried.

Celie didn't realize it was a prison at first. Tish explains that it looked like an improbable castle, built by men with small hopes and a big pile of rocks. It must have been made by the first prisoners themselves, working hard to wall themselves in. Aunt Celie looked at the wall. Walked right up to it and put her hand against a stone, leaving a damp handprint that evaporated so quick she almost forgot her name. She felt the shock of the hundreds of men penned in there.

Aunt Celie went to the drugstore, scraped her knuckles on her Levi's pulling money out of her pocket, sucked on a Coke, and thought about those men. She knew they could sense her presence, too. Every single one of them. The woman in the drugstore told her a thousand men were locked up and somebody should throw away the key, not worth a dime, the lot of them. It came to Aunt Celie in a flash they were worth more than gold, and she was destined to make one of them the jewel of them all, happy after all his suffering. Aunt Celie tested the nail polish and spun the paperback rack. She picked out the Name Your Baby book so she could look up the names of the men in the pen. The drugstore woman gave her a real sympathetic look when Celie paid for the Name Your Baby, and tossing her head toward the stone walls, asked, You here for a visit? How do you visit? Aunt Celie asked her.

The fanbelt was still on its way from Butte. Celie stayed all night in a motel painted turquoise. It must have exactly matched my ring, Aunt Tish recalls, the ring that was your Grandma Fernie's and the ring I told Celie she was to leave in my dresser drawer and she better not wear it one step outside of this house. Aunt Celie had stuck it on her pointer finger just before she took off in the Falcon.

That night Celie untied the hankies and washed them out so she'd have a fresh blouse in the morning when she followed up on her plan. She would go to the prison, she schemed, and tell them she was looking for her brother, but only knew his first name. They'd been separated as babies after their parents had been killed in a flood, maybe a fire. Celie was making a past to fit like skin. She paced around half the night in the little motel room, naked, holding a pencil, consulting her lists, her hankies drying on the shower rod. She had to decide on a first name in order to get to the second, in order to get to the man. Aunt Tish shakes her head at the logic of it. The fated one from among all those one thousand inmates. Celie reasoned that men named Sedgwick didn't get to prison and men named Thorkild deserved it. Henry would be too bald; John was in for crimes against nature, Leonard against the state. Tom stole a pig, Percy was in for larceny. Charles for bigamy, Victor for moving boundary lines, Mike for inciting a riot. Sheridan, maybe. It was a chance, a Sheridan caught for a horse thief. Yes, a horse thief would be all right. A car thief too dull. A crime of passion, as long as it was not too gruesome or too common, was what she wanted. Passion itself is a crime and he's still committing it in there, longing for me, Celie thought. She walked around her motel room, burning her image into the minds of those one thousand sleepless felons.

The next morning, sure at last of the name of her made-up brother, really her secret lover, Celie went right to the deputy warden, got right in with her clean shirt—Grandma Fernie's hankies in knots. I got a brother in here, she whispered, his name is Drake. The assistant to the absent warden was sorry, he said, no Drakes. Well, the people who took him in called him Sheridan, maybe he's enrolled under that name. Sure am sorry. I got to find him, she knew it was her last chance, her third gamble, her final wish. Grandma Fernie always called him, she hesitated as she and the warden's assistant looked down at Grandma Fernie's—or, legally, Aunt Fern's—hankies wicking moisture between her sweet breasts, and inspired, murmured the word Lacy. Grandma Fernie always called him Lacy. The name hadn't even been on her list. She nearly cried. Lacy, the deputy warden nodded, don't say. About twenty-six, you say? Yes. She hadn't, but yes, she would. What color's his hair? Celie could feel all one thousand perpetrators catch their breath and flex their restless backs. She mustn't make a mistake. She looked into her fog, trying to see the color of the hair of the brother she believed in more than God, and burst out crying, because firm and handsome as he was in her forged memory, he was wearing a hat and she couldn't see his hair. He's wearing a little hat, she sobbed. The deputy warden took it for evidence of her shattered childhood instead of a clue to her fraud, and confirmed, Lacy's your brother, all right. There's a proof, that little hat. He handed her a Kleenex, since he noted she could hardly spare a hanky. He wrote down the prisoner Lacy's last name and long number, giving her instructions to come back the next day at two.

It was all right with Aunt Celie, because first Butte forgot to send the fanbelt, and then the Greyhound misplaced it and routed it on to Seattle. At least it's a fan belt that likes to run around, Celie said to the garage man, who felt so bad about the mix-up. Aunt Celie went back to the drugstore and got some potato chips, red hots, and a Coke. The woman at the drugstore said, you got to eat good now, even though it's hot, and gave her a cheese sandwich and another Coke.

Next day at 2 p.m., Celie lined up like a visitor and felt like a movie. Someone put a scratchy cardigan over her shoulders, saying, no sense asking for trouble.

Lacy came curious to his side of the fence. He liked her free story. He liked her runaway hair. They looked at each other and both of them knew for sure they were brother and sister. His hair was common brown, she could have guessed. Lacy looked strong and innocent, just as she expected. They touched fingertips and cried and their laughter twined around each other 'til that grey place was like paradise.

That was when Aunt Celie realized she'd outsmarted herself. Aunt Fern says Celie was all hot to mate up with her inmate, but she wasn't about to commit a crime against nature. She had failed, Aunt Tish explains, in her mission to pick a pearl from among those thousand lonely men; instead, she found her long-lost and newly minted brother. Trying to fool the guards, she fooled herself.

So, with the Falcon belted and gassed again, she promised Lacy

she'd write, and came back home. Aunt Celie never got married, never
even wrote the prisoner Lacy a Christmas card, so nobody could figure
out how she came back pregnant. Had you nine months to the hour of
her visitor's pass at Deer Lodge, Aunt Tish tells me. We always said
she was your aunt to preserve her feelings and to keep you from looking among the criminal element for some Dad, our counterfeit brother.
That wouldn't be good for our girl. But Celie, Tish says admiringly,
could always take just what she was after, even through guards and
guns and dogs and stone walls. And I guess it was you she was after. I
guess it was. It was me she was after.

But Aunt Celie, when she catches me staring out the blind window,
wraps me up with her in Aunt Tish's afghan and tells me it was Aunt
Fern who ran off that summer sixteen years ago. This is what Aunt
Celie tells me. Fern always knew where she was going and headed
straight into the old calendar picture of Sedona, Arizona. It was the
calendar page facing up when Grandma Fernie died so Aunt Fern
didn't know how to turn the page, to go past it.

Karla her divorced friend was left with nothing but custody of the
nine-year-old dog, Sharp, the three-year-old boy, Geoffrey, and the
eleven-year-old van, Van. Karla didn't know which way to turn, so
Aunt Fern gave her an idea, showed her the picture, and they headed
off toward it. Aunt Fern tended Sharp, Geoff, and Van, while Karla
sulked. Every time they let Sharp out to pee, he ran off following new
scents, and they'd lose another hour. Geoff regularly threw up every
time Van turned a corner and had to be bathed and soothed back from
motion sickness. Aunt Fern used baking soda and psychology and a
road atlas. Van lost its ability to go in reverse, which was hard on
Geoff because it caused more turning, but was a sign to Aunt Fern to
keep going and keep taking care. She missed Grandma Fernie so much
she still needed to nurse anything sick.

Aunt Fern's still like that, nursing everything: even the African violets so fussy they kill themselves if they even touch a drop of the very
water they need to drink, even the cranky lawnmower that pitches

parts of itself across the yard, even me when she mashed strawberries for me when I had tonsillitis.

But next thing they knew they were smack up against Cathedral Rock and Aunt Fern said, this is where I get off. I can't listen to anything louder than a stone, and put her hands over her ears when Karla said she didn't know who had used her more, that worthless guy Eddie, or Fern, who hadn't paid a dollar on Van's gas. Karla herself had no business in some red rocks. She left Aunt Fern by the side of the road, waving to Geoff and Sharp. Aunt Fern turned around and suddenly, just like Aunt Celie had, she felt like she was in a movie. At least maybe a commercial. She listened to the red rocks, the curled scorpions, the tenacious plants, until all of them were too noisy. She climbed the rocks until her own blood was dry, red dust. With just a little more effort she would petrify. Aunt Celie calls her the rolling stone every time she takes off to visit some scene she admires in a magazine.

Still, Aunt Fern in trying to be a rock was actually turning them over, looking for something human. Maybe a man who would not jangle her reverie. Maybe her mom.

She discovered the old Indian graveyard and set up her camp in the cemetery, taking turns sleeping on each grave, her ear to the ground. Any grave too talkative, she'd get up and move in the middle of the night until she found one sufficiently quiet. In the morning, Tish says, Fern examined the tracery of her sleep like hieroglyphs of the spectral conversations left in the red dust. All our socks, Aunt Celie remembers, came back pink and would never bleach white again. We thought she was trying to hear from your Grandma Fernie, who was one-quarter blood herself, through those graves. But your Grandma Fernie was always quiet; even when she was alive she never said much.

Fern slept there until she thought the old Indians would talk her ear off and she thought she might as well be at home. They almost sucked the air out of her just so they could keep talking. Before she left, I guess it was the bones under the ground gave her a present. Or maybe Grandma Fernie saw to it that those dead Indians gave Fern a little drawing of a person inside her, just like on the stones. I don't know,

they were not her tribe. And really old. Anyway, Aunt Fern came home
pregnant. We never wanted to tell you, Aunt Tish confides, because
we didn't want our little girl trying to find a daddy in a boneyard, not
even among magic petroglyphs. That was really what Fern went out to
get from that calendar page; it was you, my girl.
    It was me she wanted.

Grandaddy shuffles around the aunts and they dose him by the
spoonful with sweet words and chicken gravy. All the rest of us eat
little cups of yogurt and it really makes Grandaddy angry. He's afraid
we'll slip yogurt into his mashed potatoes. He caught Aunt Tish at it
once, he says.

This is what Aunt Fern says, pulling the book out of my hand and
snapping it shut without a marker, crawling into midnight bed with
me to tell me it was Aunt Tish, left alone in the house that summer sixteen years ago, left alone with the screen door banging, flies knocking
into the windows, and her heart beating. Tish had to streak her hair
and bake her flesh with bottle sunshine, Aunt Fern says, because of
staying indoors. Aunt Tish wouldn't go out for the mail, the movies,
or the Fourth of July. Wouldn't go out for ice cream, she was tied to
the telephone like chains. She watched the fireworks from the tiny attic window and felt like two movies, like she was in black-and-white
and the sky was in color.
    She ate the nasturtiums she could reach from the porch railing. She
coaxed me to try that, too, hanging by my knees, without using my
hands. She can still do it. Tish wore her cutoff shorts, measuring to get
the legs exactly even, pulling threads from one side and then the other.
She couldn't go out until she got them even, she said, and ran out of
material before she ran out of summertime, snipping her scissors, pulling threads, 'til there was little left to quarrel over, with a difference,
Aunt Fern says, only Tish herself could discern.
    She'd wait for the phone to ring. She'd listen to any offer, alumi-
num siding, any prize she won, ten free bowling lessons. Put my name

down, Tish said, but wouldn't go out of the house to stick her fingers
in the face of a bowling ball. She was even polite to the kids who called
to say the refrigerator was running and Prince Albert was in a can. The
real reason she wouldn't leave was because of the Wrong Number.
Who became the insistent caller. Who became the only breath in the
house. Her Wrong Number persisted, calling at odd hours in a cast of
characters, a dozen voices. The voice started out as an obscene call designed to shock, but it made Tish laugh. Then the voice called back as
the president. Then a swami, then Gregory Peck, Bette Davis, Bugs
Bunny, a leprechaun, the next-door neighbor, even as a fortune cookie.
I would like to have heard that one.

Anyway, it was the day after Independence Day and a storm rose
over the mountains, belittling the fireworks of the night before. Tish
answered the phone on the first ring. The caller was doing another
fancy voice, making Tish laugh, telling jokes about Heaven in the
voice of God. Aunt Tish was very interested in the Heaven jokes, always hoping to get news of her mother. Then the phone crackled, the
maple tree around the corner got a big lightning gouge in it, and the
line was broken. I can still see a trace of that lightning strike. We've all
put our hands into that old wound, where the tree went smooth with
fire that night. We never told you, Aunt Fern says, because we didn't
want you to reach for the phone every time it rings, expecting a dad to
call you up, it's no way to live. I actually heard once that the Virgin
Mary got pregnant from the Dove talking in her ear, but we're Protes-
tants. That caller with all those voices never called again. Tish never
needed to hear another word. The caller had told her everything.

It was me.

Grandaddy doesn't go to work any more, so the aunts send him after newspapers and thread. Otherwise, now that he doesn't get to go
off with his lunchbox, he sits on the porch still trying to puzzle out
which one of his bad girls is the worst. They bring his lunch out to him
in the old lunchbox.

I don't mind being as pure as Jesus. Maybe more pure: not only no dad, not even a mom. But I think I'll get out of this house, get a guy, and get a baby the regular way. But now Grandaddy's started following me around, thinking he can keep it from happening to me. Whatever it was that happened.

The three aunts, Celie, Fern, and Tish, puffed up all at once, like a sudden magician's bouquet. It nearly killed Grandaddy to have three—he didn't say the word *pregnant*—daughters. He claimed he would have killed any one of them who got herself knocked up, but with all three wearing smocks, a man couldn't kill three women, and three little ones, he said, if he let his mind follow up. Where are my cousins, you ask? Well, my aunts fooled Grandaddy. Only one was pregnant. Only one shell hid the pea. The other two were pretending just so Grandaddy couldn't kill the ripe one, couldn't kill her or banish her or pick on her. He didn't know which way to aim his shotgun, not a suitor in sight, his three girls puking, then sucking ice. Then his three girls gnawing on raw potatoes, then chewing licorice, then eating bread and jam, bacon and eggs, eating him out of house and home. Then his three girls learning to knit and his three girls packing up toothbrushes and layettes.

They took off in the Falcon, late one night. We still have a picture of that car, with the aunts all young, all legs and hair and laughing, draped all over it. Don't call at the hospital, they ordered him, we're going to another town so there'll be no gossip. They liked being the only news that spring, but they wouldn't submit to being mere gossip. Paint the spare room, they ordered him. We'll come home to a nursery. Grandaddy was ashamed at the hardware store to ask for pink or blue, so he cleverly asked for yellow. And yellow my room still is.

It was bright as a daffodil when the three thin-again daughters came home with one basket, one baby, three big smiles, six swollen and leaking paps, Fern brags. Grandaddy asked, who lost, who's grieving, whose is this? And all three said, I'm her aunty and you're her grandaddy. Then Grandaddy realized he'd been tricked by three evil daughters. Only one of those gals had strayed and the other two just

pretended, to protect the bad one. He watched all bird-eyed, but couldn't figure whether Celie, Fern, or Tish was the real momma. I'll get a knife, then, and divide it up in three parts, he threatened. We didn't fall for that old ploy, Aunt Tish says, there was no wisdom in it. Grandaddy complained, you all paraded around town in those hatching jackets without the sense to be ashamed, but not one of you hags will own up to being a mother. There's not a creature on earth behaves this way. You gals are witches and this child's an orphan. Three aunts can't equal one mother, and that's the last he said. Grandaddy's new name rattled off their sharp little tongues, and the baby, that was me, changed them all into aunts.

And here I am.

And Grandaddy thinks if he figures out which aunt's a mom, then he'll be happy. What he's forgotten is that whichever one he chooses, he'll still be stuck with a riddle. If he decides which aunt got me, he still won't know where I came from. The aunties think their daddy is a cross to bear, so not one of them would have inflicted a dad on me.

I sit with Grandaddy on the porch swing and he raps me on the knees with his newspaper when I swing too hard. So I tell him what I think. It's this. The aunts missed their mom so much, my Grandma Fernie, they just thought such mom thoughts they had a miracle and got a baby. You ought to be caned, Grandaddy says, whopping me with the rolled-up newspaper.

=◇=

"Coach with the Six Insides"

—Finnegans Wake

LIKE A BUS. From the outside you would think it was a bus, Mother almost whispered. Tuesday. Stand by the mailboxes by 9 a.m. not to miss it. It will stop just for you. Don't stand too close to the highway. Get way over in the weeds. Then when you step inside that little bus, Mother promised, it will be a whole library, more than you could read in ten years.

Korey tried to figure how to unfold a library from the six planes of the container, the bus. Mother could fold a fan and a swan and a box out of newspaper. A box has six sides, she told Korey as they colored large numbers, and that's how you play dice. She taught Korey to make roses out of toilet paper, poking them in their hair with bobby pins. The puffs of flowers stayed in Mother's luxuriant hair all day; the first time Korey forgot and moved her head they slipped off. But how had Mother come up with this new knowledge, even this word, Bookmobile? And how did she know where to stand? And when?

Mother went through Korey's hair with a rat-tail comb and said, I'll walk you half way. Jaggly Point Road took a long stretch and two unaccountable twists before it gave out, spitting gravel onto the paving of Township Highway. But before the first curve, Mother turned back to circle round through the woods, where she looked for mushrooms she cooked in butter and didn't let anybody else taste. Never know, she'd say with practically every bite. Come the whole way, Korey begged, but Mother left her to walk by herself, to unfold the Bookmobile on her own.

She waited by the mailboxes, just as Mother told her. The weeds prickled her legs and grabbed at her shirt. She picked foxgloves and put them in her mailbox, putting up the flag for the mailman. Every day they'd peek in, expecting just about anything to be waiting for them in the shadow of the mailbox, the arched temple of correspondence. Korey loved to put the flag up to signal the mailman, pick up this mail. And let the flag down to tell the world, got the mail. One time they got a package so big the mailman had to hang it by its twine to the outside. Mother struggled with that package all the way home, got a catch in her side teasing Korey about what it might be from Mother's own grandmother, an old woman in a tiny picture on Mother's dresser. Just dishrags, that's what she sent me once. Dishrags threaded with satin ribbon so they looked like bloomers. When they got home, Mother took a long time to undo the twine so she could use it again, and tearing back the brown paper they found hazelnuts and hand-sewn doll dresses and a smoked ham.

Finally a bus came and went right on past. It slammed to a stop way past the mailboxes and on the other side of the road. Korey was standing on the wrong side. A pair of glasses and a mouth leaned out the window and hollered, you waiting to come to the Bookmobile? Cross on over. Mother had told Korey to stand by the mailboxes, not across from them. And down a piece. What if she was wrong about the books in the bus? Korey left the comforting shadow of the mailbox with her own last name.

Why did the chicken cross the road? she once asked Mother, and ever since Mother liked to ask it herself. Korey flapped across the yellow line and peeked around the front of the bus. She worried how to get from the bus on the outside to a real library on the inside. The door parted with a gasp of air. Korey took a giant step and pulled herself up into the bus. The pair of glasses and twitching mouth bent down to her.

Where is your library card? Are you big enough to use a library? Can you read words yet? Korey looked around. It was a playhouse library made out of a schoolbus. Korey didn't have a library card. But Mother said I could, and warned the Bookmobile driver, Mother says I

can read words long as your arm. And even though it wasn't a real library like in town, she was going to read every last book in the bus.

You can check them out, Mother had explained. So Korey explained it all to the lady, that she would take home books and read them for a week and bring them back when the Bookmobile would come again, on a Tuesday at 9 a.m., stopping at the mailboxes. Children's books at the back, the lady pointed. Korey reached tentatively for a green book with gilded ivy on its spine. Too old for you, said the lady, the buttons on her dress bright as eyes. Korey turned to another shelf and reached for a fat book with *Secret* in the title. No, no, no, no, said the book lady; the bus rocked as she hurried toward Korey. How old are you? Six and a half. Then you may choose only from this shelf. But first we have to fill out your request for a library card. She looked dubiously from the form to Korey, but the girl recited an answer to every question. You can write your name, I suppose? And there she had her. I can only write in printing, Korey admitted. It will do, said the lady, rubbing her finger behind her glasses.

Korey returned to her allotted shelf of thin, ragged picture books. These are just baby books, she said to herself. It's your age group, said the book lady who would not let her pull out any of the others. Well, they were pretty enough, Korey would take them. She began to stack the books to take home.

Only two. Only two. The book lady shook the bus. Because your library card isn't ready yet. Korey gave up all but two books with pretty pictures of castles and beetles. I'll reshelve, said the lady, you may know how to read, but I doubt you know the Dewey Decimal System. You leave that to me. She stamped the due date and made Korey sign her name on the cards she pulled from pockets at the back of each book. Printing will do. Snapping them up to keep her from looking too long at other children's names, the book lady stood the cards on their heads in a file box. She held the borrowed books while Korey climbed down out of the bus. Now you keep these clean and keep them up from the dog. She drove away, dust billowing over Korey, books, foxgloves, and the road signs.

Korey could not read as well as Mother, who could read a whole story in a word. Once, when the mailbox had been empty, and as they were turning back toward the two twists and then the long stretch, Mother had pointed up at the road signs. Jaggly and Township, she said, were two crooks who met right here, one dragging a bagful of diamonds and the other a kidnapped girl. They were about to trade them. But both of them, Jaggly and Township, had been followed by the law. The girl was so mad to be snatched before she had her lunch, she kicked really hard and split open the bag. Diamonds went every whichyway. When the crooks stooped over to pick them up, the law caught up with them, jumped on their backs, and whacked them both on top of the head. Right here. Jaggly and Township resisted arrest and fought to the end rather than give it up and rot in jail and their names became roads. Mother's story took them home in no time, even with no letter to open when they got there. Even with them having to stop and fling themselves down to show the way the crooks fell with the bloody head of one in the bloody lap of the other, a map of how the roads came to be the way they are, with the head of one twisted road in the lap of the other sprawling one. They got home in no time, even with having to stop and examine a rock now and then to make sure it wasn't an overlooked diamond.

Korey went home from the Bookmobile, sat importantly on the bird's-eye maple chair in the exact middle of the kitchen, and read her books, sitting cross-legged on one book while she read the other. Mother chided her, why did you get such baby books, you already read them in ten minutes, now you have nothing for the rest of the week. You should get books that will take a whole week long to read. Korey thought of the fat book with the word *Secret* in the title.

She told Mother about the lady and her rules. I'll put the books on top of the icebox, Mother said, setting them out of Korey's reach on the refrigerator. And Korey went back to reading the familiar words in the kitchen, Hotpoint, July, Left Rear, Left Front, Right Rear, Right Front, Bake, Off, On, Frigidaire, Hot, Cold. Mother pulled the chair over to the calendar and let Korey put circles around all the Tuesdays. Then Korey made circles around all the other days, too, so they wouldn't feel left out.

The next week Mother said she'd go along and set that librarian straight about her reading levels. On their way down Jaggly Point Road, a garter snake slithered across a sunny patch. Mother stopped him with a stone. Caught under the boulder, his fine, striped head writhed, his tongue flicking. Look, Mother said, and pulled Korey close. They both squatted by the snake pinned under the stone. Look

at his tongue, she called it forked. How did Mother know how to torture him to get him to stick it out and quiver it at them? She let go of
the picture books and they splayed out on the road.

Mother picked up the books and dusted them on her behind. They
went on to meet Township Highway. Mother stood opposite the
mailboxes and a ways down. The Bookmobile stopped directly in
front of them. Mother lifted Korey into the bus and handed back the
baby books. Korey bragged to the lady, Mother killed a snake. She was
not one bit afraid.

She waited for Mother to tell the book lady that they could have
any of the big books and as many as they could carry. But Mother
hung back. Tell me what you'd like to read about, the lady bent down.
Thinking fast, Korey said, I want to read about those two crooks,
Jaggly and Township. The book lady, who drove a whole library all
day long, knew nothing of them. Mother told me they were crooks and
when they were shot their blood got all over the diamonds and the girl.
It took two weeks of boiling water and lye soap to get the girl clean but
money is something that never can come clean, she quoted Mother's
tale. And they made the roads just how the crooks fell down. Korey
flung herself down in the pattern of Jaggly Point Road and the Bookmobile jiggled. Mother stood with her back to them, running her hand
along the books.

Your library card isn't processed yet, the book lady said. But you
can still check out two books from this shelf. The bus wobbled as she
went toward the picture books. Oh, that's okay, mumbled Mother, I
think we're moving into town, anyway, and pulled Korey from the
Bookmobile. They checked their empty mailbox and looked for the
snake on the way home, but couldn't find him.

=◇=

Hamlet's Planets
Parable 2:B

O God, I could be bounded in a nutshell and count myself a King of infinite space, were it not that I have bad dreams.

—*Hamlet*, act 2, scene 2

THE WOMAN SLID her red-enameled thumbnail into the soft fiber that sealed the bottom of the walnut shell. She twisted her nail a sharp quarter-turn and the walnut shell divided. The two halves quivered in her palm like upturned tortoises. Then she looked into them.

One half revealed a little man, covered up with a quilt, sucking his thumb. The other half had been painted by what appeared to have been an apprentice miniaturist who was himself a miniature. The dome of the walnut shell was decorated with tiny, blue five-pointed stars, mythological figures in gauzy gowns, sun, moon, and winds, all with solemn faces; a band of the figures of the zodiac crossed the little heaven, and a god in a cloud, labeled with the tetragrammaton, pointed his blessings and admonitions.

In the other walnut half, the little man stirred. His quilt was finely embroidered with herbs and blossoms. The woman could see the detail of rosemary, fierce little thoughtful faces on the pansies, fennel, tall-stemmed columbines along the sides, rue, daisies looking to the sun along the top border, and one odd little cluster of violets with withered petals, trailing a few threaded purple smudges at the bottom of the quilt like broken blossoms on a forest floor. The quilt was the most beautiful piece of needlework the woman had ever seen. The

little man held in his hand (the one that was not being sucked) a crown that looked like it had been carved out of a single piece of ivory or bone. It bore no jewels, only an elaborately engraved 𝕴.

The man took his thumb from his mouth, opened his eyes, and glared at the woman. "Vile dream," he said.

"I am not your dream," she responded. "I was shelling walnuts. You came with the rest, from a tree in my aunt's back yard. You belong merely to this season's harvest."

"How long have you been a gravemaker?" asked the little man.

"I am only making apple cakes," she responded.

"A player gravemaker," he began, fitting the crown to his head and speaking more to himself. "I grant you your jawbone once more, Yorick; I shall be your tongue and your grin, and you yet shall be my crowner."

"I do not believe you are Hamlet," said the woman. "You are more like a little nutmeat masquerading, playing at Hamlet with sham props (although a lovely quilt). You lack the tone, the rhythms, the poetry of the true Hamlet."

"The true Hamlet was a willful player merely, madam. And you are more a fool than a clown; though you dig my grave and disturb my sleep, you are but a shadow, a bad dream."

"I'm not. Did you paint your ceiling yourself?"

"Like an Italian I lay on my back on a scaffold and colored a universe."

"Like a woman making dreams. If you were really Hamlet you would have made something more of that last speech."

"I have lost my will, now I have nothing but you, a poor fool compared with Lear's. You do nothing but play the part of the woman, another compendium of Os. You dream me poorly, madam."

"You can't switch plays and you can't make me an object of your dream."

"Neither can you deny me my dreams, even bad ones."

"What shall I do with you?" she asked, her fingers throbbing.

"Plant me. Just don't ask me to say, 'Wretched queen, adieu, I am dead, report me and my cause aright to the unsatisfied . . .'"

"I am the unsatisfied. You are not dead. I am not the queen. This is not a tragedy—you don't die. You are too insubstantial; you yourself are but a dream from the unbounding of my nutshell."

"Our universes have collided then. We quarrel over our wandering

stars," and he gazed toward the memory of his little handpainted ceiling, once above him, now beside him.

"Who will tell us what this show meant?" she quoted softly.

"Ah, now to show the play is to play the show. Our meaning's lost in the making."

"I am going to seal you up again."

"Fine. Goodbye, Dream, I sleep again."

"I am not your dream. 'You are naught. I'll mark the play—'"

"You disturb another man's bones," he said emphatically.

"It is the manner of dreams."

"Not to poorly quote."

"To poorly paint?" she taunted, holding the dome of his shell over his head, shadowing his little bed.

"For the time—" he began, but the woman sealed the shell shut with her bloodred fingernail polish and set him on the shelf. She thought about planting him.

=◇=

To Speak
and to Keep Silent

Responding to a riddle:

Here I am, caught between.

Between persons on both sides of the pages.

On one side, my readers tempt me to talk about parable. What is a parable? they ask. These stories are not about the Kingdom of Heaven, are they? I'm not supposed to catch some secret meaning from them, am I?

Well, whenever anyone asks me a riddle, I fall for it: What is a parable? We'll risk our necks to come up with why the fireman wears red suspenders or what it is that goes on four legs, then two, then three.

But on the other side, some of the characters in this book resent an afterword. They are dismayed that a storyteller will stoop to talk *about* story. And to tell tales on us, they complain, since we've been so close. Especially, they say, since it might perpetuate the lie that nonfiction has more authority than fiction.

How can I honor the appeal of the residents on both sides of the page?

To speak and to keep silent.

"It's as though you are gossiping about us. It's not done," scolds Olivia, reminding me as she reminded Robert, "Never, dear, look for morals after you find out riddles."

Oh, but Olivia Sweet, parables don't look for morals. A parable—or a riddle—is not a cautionary tale, not an allegory or pretend-story that hides its daggery ideas in narrative cloaks.

"You tell us, then, dear. What is it?"

Even wise Olivia, who lives in a parable and can conjure one from her teacup, cannot define it. It won't do, I sense, to remind her that parable shares its etymological roots with *parabola*. I shrug, a parable is a shapely story. Told on a curve.

"There you have it," Olivia taps her fine old handbag. But she glances away, veiling her disappointment at my simplistic response.

Well, it is simple enough to explain that etymologically *parabollein* means 'to throw beside,' whereas *symbollein* is 'to throw together' and *emballein* 'to throw in.' Thus, parable narrowly avoids the collisions that lodge in what we call symbol or emblem, those forms all thrown together down one well, drenched in too much meaning. Parable skirts equivalences, leaves us hanging by its loop.

We will not slip free unless we answer the riddle: What is a parable? It can't be any harder than, say, *What has an eye but cannot see, a long tail but no feet?* It can't be any easier, though, than *Why did the chicken cross the road?* Did Samson become a parable when he asked the riddle, *Out of the eater came something to eat, out of the strong came something sweet?* In every puzzle, as with Samson's riddle in the Book of Judges, even bees in a lion's carcass, even deception between lovers, is the revelation of uncanny resemblances among death and sex and strength and loss and honey and the starry sky and the fluidity of language. Maybe the only way to slip free from the mortal consequences of riddle is to slip into nearby parable.

Parable is not a genre:

Let's turn a page.

Must we be able to tell a parable in a single breath? No. If Jesus had used pencils, his parables would have been longer. Well, must we be able to inscribe a parable in the palm of a hand? No. If a parable could be grasped, then Nizami's Majnun would not have gone mad, pursuing his beloved Layla as letters of the alphabet, Night, wilderness, the animals, God, and the grave. Is a parable an optical illusion? Maybe. If Krishna had not loaned his own eye to Arjuna in the Bhagavad Gita, we would think parable was merely a matter of illumination.

Okay. Parables are not allegories, not ideas in nightgowns, pageants of virtues and vices appearing as gauzy ladies. In parable, a nightgown and an idea might take up nearly the same gauzy space; one drapes a body, the other drapes the shadow of a body. An allegory tells its secrets, but a parable makes them up and keeps them.

Okay. Parables are not moral fables, those foxes and geese with warning labels sewed to their vests. What is the art of reading if we want explanations, biographies, morals, theories from outside the story? Yet parable is a story that loves theories, as well as foxes and geese.

Okay. Parables are not theologies, those systems that devour their own myths by attempting to suppress its images and force the sacred to speak prudently. Theology erases images; parable draws in the dark.

I could be fond of detective stories, were they not so fond of single

causes and corpses; I could revere the proverb, if it did not make its
straight so narrow; I could cling to the making of histories, were it not
for the conquests and the literalism; I would love philosophy if it were
not for the laws of noncontradiction; I would turn to the fairy tale,
were it not for the scarcity of third brothers on white horses.

Okay. Parables may resemble games. A parable is like a field with a
bone hidden in it, or a dark closet with a lost pearl. Fictional people
harvest their field and watch the sunset behind it. The bone does not
intrude upon their narrative lives. They hide their old photographs or
throw their wet mittens in the closet. But they never discover the pearl.
A narrative field is not a mere field, as in a game; a game closet con-
tains game pearls that are counters or stations necessary to the game
and only to the game. Closets in stories, though, open onto psyche's
rooms and contents. A game's field—no matter how iconically dotted
with ideas of bones, plants, footprints—is abstract, is its set of instructions. The story's field is more than a game of discovery or
equivalences, it is in language both tangible and transcendent. What
if a reader catches the gleam of the bone in the field or the pearl stuck
in the crack in the closet? A reader may purloin the bone or the pearl
from the story, yet the story goes on just the same—sunsets, wet mittens. Or does it?

Does it matter that there is an unopened birthday present in one of
these stories, an inaccessible book embellished with gilt ivy in another?
Might they be out of reach of readers, writers, and characters, yet are
necessary to the story? If a pearl is caught within a narrative closet, it is
a narrative pearl, whether it is discovered or not. So in what way does
the pearl come to exist in the universe of the reader? As the reader
brings to consciousness the closet, photographs, wet mittens, the
reader also brings into consciousness the possibility of the pearl in that
closet of the psyche. The story exists only by telling or reading: what is

less clear is that the story generates the life of the reader or teller, giving to the reader or teller—by resonance and by metaphor—unknown bones, secreted pearls.

Okay. A parable is, if anything at all, a riddle. Aristotle defined riddle as the expression of true facts under impossible combinations. He explained that this expression cannot be accomplished by any arrangement of ordinary words, but it can by the use of metaphor. Giving the greatest praise to metaphor, he claimed the mark of genius is to have an eye for resemblances. In a parable, the eye-to-eye conversation between readers and characters is the expression of true facts under impossible combinations. And these persons on both sides of the page get along by their own collaborative metaphors, by their resemblances, by their own parabolic genius. They loop the familiar with the strange, distort the familiar into the uncanny in the miraculous geometry of the parable wherein the characters touch the reader at one point, the writer at another.

Okay. Parable is almost in myth's dark folds. Myth is a deep pocket full of the seeds of reality. Parable pokes a hole in the pocket, spilling from wisdom to question, turning out authority for the sake of desire. John Dominic Crossan distinguishes myth from parable by telling us that parable is in subversive tension with myth; that parable, unlike myth, is a fiction designed for change, not reassurance.

Finally, then, in this catalogue of approximate genres, parable is myth's shadow. Myth invents time, though it inhabits eternity. Parables are more modest: they exist next door to death. Myths create the cultures that invent the myths; reality is a paper-folding trick.

Drilling deep down into the mythic psyche that seemed, once upon a time, to provide the masterplots of Western consciousness, parables cut trajectories across old, shattered stories. But in our time of decaying and competing myths, we ride upon something more ephemeral—

parables. Although the end and beginning of a millennium may itself be the only myth we share in this liminality of fragmented and rejected systems, we come to read (to know) by the lens of parable and paradox. If we must know myths in order to read parables—in order to drop the eccentric, ironic, iconoclastic tiny stories into the chasm of great and deep tales—then our dilemma may be that of amnesia. Today, we rattle around among incoherent fragments of Vishnu's dream, Coca-Cola, Star Man, Chuang Tzu's butterfly, the shopping channel, the Corn Maiden, the Net and the Web, Christ's passion, Cupid's arrow, Jacob's ladder. Still, those crumpled myths and ephemeral shards have their power. And perhaps they are as sufficient as what we imagine to have been an integrated worldview. If parables cut across the grain of larger stories, how do parables function in a time when the larger stories—myths—are collapsing or converging or forgotten? Perhaps it makes myth possible again. And perhaps even the least of stories affirms the universe we are telling into existence.

Nor is parable a matter of interpretation:

Looking on the other side of the page.

Years ago, I came across an old book, a narrow and soiled red suede, stamped with the title *Essay on Silence*. It opened to a quire of blank pages. I never bothered to find out that Fra Elbertus was the playful pseudonym of an Arts & Crafts fine printer and homespun philosopher, an artist who drowned at sea. It seems now that Elbert Hubbard, the man behind the joke, produced his best writing in *Essay on Silence*. My childself did not see the joke. The empty, gilt-edged pages seemed to me not amusing but mysterious. Perhaps ever after reading that blank book, I have desired to write so well.

The only mark in that book we could call writing is the elegant

translucent watermark of his press, Roycroft. No, wait. I mean, the only writing is in some penciled curlicues on the latter pages by a small scribe on the verge of deciphering the alphabet's code. The scribbles keep the pages blank. No, wait. I mean, the only writing must be on the first page of the little book, long ago ripped out. A love note? A grocery list? Maybe the drawing of a mouse.

Formalists will never let authors or readers intrude on their sacred textual space. Conversely, historians of literature stay safely beside the point. Postmodernists—under the name of readers in any generation—take over and make over any text they touch. The rest of us, in our encounters with Heathcliff or Heraclitus, keep turning over the same words: *I am Heathcliff* still blows across the heather of Penistone Hill; *It is in changing that things find rest* still moves contemplation. And we keep looking for another note, like a scrap torn from the pages of Heathcliff's heart, the soul of Heraclitus. How, then, is a parable distinguishable from a novel or aphorism; how is a fictional demonlover distinguishable from a fictionalized philosopher? To locate the distinctions that sit counterpoint to the resemblances is to perform a parable. The accident in the story is the intention of the plot; the catastrophe within the narrative is the ceremony of the narrative. A story's sense is embedded in metaphor and cannot be translated to mere unequivocal discourse. The story tells its own curly tale. Yet, a page can be ripped from a blank book, confounding its own silence.

Does this mean, a reader asks suspiciously, that I am not invited to interpret?

Not at all; parable, I would concede, is more a means of interpretation than it is a genre. Even the same story is not always the same genre. Form changes by inflection. Character is as fluid as plot within the same set of words. Every tale is as mutable as the deceptively simple Parable of the Sower. In parable neither genre, typology, nor ideological envelope captures the narrative, the casting of the seed.

A matter of participation:

Turning another page.

So, what is a parable, if it is not in the shape of the tale or the mind of the reader?

Last night I abandoned this riddle and went to sleep. I dreamed my friend came over with his child, the one he has only in this dream. He sat on a wooden chair all worried while the child played on the floor and my husband and I played in bed. He was troubled over a song he had composed, unable to remember the words. He scolded us for staying in bed (we were like puppies under the down comforter), as he wanted desperately for us to help him write another song, using all of the words of the first song so impossible to remember. He could then sing the new song of the same words in order to remember the elusive one. We explained with dream logic that he suffered the affliction of Parallel Memory. We recalled words to the song we had never heard, the words the composer himself had forgotten. I interrupted to suggest, oh, why don't you just go out there on stage and say, now for my next number . . . five . . . and play one note and sing the word *five*. And now for my next number . . . nine.

My dreamself was no funnier in dreamtime than I would have been in waking time. And my dream demanded explication. Remember the old joke about jokes? Telling the same old jokes over and over, friends came to know the jokes so well that they numbered them and simply called out the mnemonic numbers to one another, with rounds and rounds of laughter. The fool of the joke came along, watched for awhile puzzled, and finally shouted out, twenty-three! And no one laughed. When he asked why, the jokemasters patronized the fool, well, some people just can't tell a joke.

I awoke from the dream a little chagrined that even asleep I couldn't tell a joke, or that my dreamself would use such an old chestnut to torment my dreamfriend who was afflicted with this dream malady, Parallel Memory. And I finally realized I was the one who was trying to recover the elusive words from a forgotten melody. It was as though I thought I could answer the riddle of parable by finding the same words from outside the parables to repeat the parables themselves. It was I who was afflicted with this 'parallel memory,' the error of paraphrase or explanation. Add to those irksome explainers of jokes and repeaters of movies and reporters of dreams, add the fool who tries to confound the riddle of parable, which is, after all, a narrative way of keeping the silence.

Readers ask me to speak.

Characters want me to keep silent.

Well, what is it that the parable wants?

Freud's famous reiteration of the old riddle, *what is it that a woman wants?* disguised what Freud himself wanted: dreams, jokes, to peel back memories, to show desire itself. But Freud kept forgetting, repressing, what he wanted—which was story, not relief from story. His own storytelling, his own narrative pulse, always betrayed his phallic success story, his theoretical purgations of fantasy, his attempts to rescue us from what he took to be our childhood illness of religion. Riddles (sieves) and parables defy our attempts to own them, but they grant us the wish of giving back to parable what it wants. That is its loop. Parable is the story that keeps sifting through our fingers; who knows where it will fall.

A king wiser than Freud once earned his way through a story by keeping his vow (by becoming his word) and by solving riddles (by breaking through word) put to him by a vampire residing in the corpse he carried over his shoulder. When the vampire—and ultimately the god Shiva—offered the king anything he desired (the most treacherous riddle of all), the king's wish was: May all the ravishing, wonderful tales I heard from the vampire be remembered and cherished. He desired the story, not to conquer story.

So what are these little stories doing calling themselves parables? Parable offers no cure. Solving the riddle is no salvation. Parables—those stories that talk back—are both cause and remedy of the amnesia of self: a story bursts through the amnesiac cloud of this stranger we call self. The story is a mirror. Yet, a parabolic experience is a disjunction from the familiar self; it contributes to the fictionalizing of self. The mirror shatters. A writer certainly is more intimate with her characters than with her readers; who of them satisfy more of the criteria for fiction? Parables also address another amnesia, the one caused by a certitude of self. The story is not a mirror, after all. If these two—our stranger and our familiar selves—are to be celebrated rather than overcome, does the parable raise the specter of "nothing is real" except as text—whether metaphysical or aesthetic? Then how can I believe in my work or my valentine? The riddle that asks, *If love is an invention, how can I trust love?* fails to consider how I, an inventor of that love, am also an invention, a fiction. Our culture has emphasized for a generation that gender is a social construct. In these last, angry huffs of patriarchy, what could possibly be the politics of our apolitical and playful stories unless they extend the assertion with a question? If the self is a reverie, then who or what dreams? A koan, cousin to a parable, is an exchange designed to empty the mind. Our cultural questions are designed to empty our presuppositions. We are living in a parabolic curve that questions all manner of selves.

The parabolic curve traces fault lines on the planet, draws comic or tragic grimaces, follows the line of a frog's hop, folds into hand's clasp, feels the galaxy's spin. We write out of a desire to read the story we crave; the story emerges in the grasp of its own desire. Hamlet went

to sleep in a nutshell world, homemade and infinite, to confront his bad dreams, to compose his own essay on silence. His lips, like his firmament and nest, are sealed. Hubbard's little *Essay on Silence,* the blank pages I read so intently when I was a child, was made up from paper trimmings and sold for thirty cents in stamps. Soon after the turn of the century, someone slipped a calling card between the loosened suede cover and endpage of their little pretend book that eventually made its way to me. Near century's turn again, I pull out the card and look at the script, at the die-cut edges of the card. The blankest book could keep us up a thousand and one nights.

Chatterboxes in these stories protest: why is it necessary to call our own little tales parables? Perhaps to honor my readers, whose risks are complex and creative. "Ah, that's it, at last," Olivia turns, satisfied. The souls within the stories get faraway looks; I think they are just beginning to consider the enchanting ones separated from them and connected to them only by this alphabet world. Thanks for asking me the riddle. To those on both sides of these thin pages, I offer my gratitude.

=◇=